CRAZY RICH REDNECKS

A SWEET SOUTHERN ROMANTIC COMEDY

KACI LANE

Copyright © 2022 by Kaci Lane

All rights reserved.

This is a work of fiction. Names, characters, organizations, places, events and incidents are either products of the author's imagination or are used fictitiously. Any resemblance to actual persons, living or dead, or actual events is purely coincidental.

No part of this work may be reproduced, or stored in a retrieval system, or transmitted in any form by any means without written permission from the author.

CRAZY RICH REDNECKS

CHAPTER ONE

Mackenzie

"Not another Hallmark movie." I groan and swipe my hands down my face.

If I have to direct one more sappy love story between a widower and a bakery owner, I'm changing careers.

"Mack, Hallmark has been your bread and butter."

I laugh. The irony in Arnie's statement is uncanny. If I had a dime for every baked good on set—both for props and from craft services—I could retire today. The silver lining is I can turn down any sweet in a second, since I have constant access to an abundance of sugar.

"I just need a change from directing second-chance romance scenes in subzero temperatures." I slump back in the zebra-print office chair. The padding is almost as thin as my patience with low-budget romances.

Arnie sighs and wipes a hand over his balding head. "How about a reality show?"

"Ha!" I slap the armrest, then rub my palm. The arms have even less padding. "Have you forgotten who I am?"

Because I haven't. I'm the same girl who dreamed of creating difference-making documentaries as a kid. Reality TV would be the death of me.

"It's not what you're thinking. This is a baking show."

"Like one of those competitions?" My stomach sours as I envision a dozen or so people frosting cakes in an all-white commercial kitchen.

"No. A miniseries focusing on a woman who makes custom cookies."

I wrinkle my forehead. A one-woman cookie show? Now I'm more confused than ever.

Arnie's gray eyebrows pull together. As my only agent of ten years and my mom's friend for much longer than that, he can read me like the main characters in his favorite movie script.

"It's featuring a small-town cookie baker's recipes during the holidays. They plan on shooting it this Christmas, then showing it next year."

I twist my mouth. "Wait, small-town cookie baker?" I laugh. "How is that not Hallmark?"

"Because it's a real woman in a real small town. Besides, she's been married almost forty years, so you won't have to worry about sappy love stories."

I squint. Did I say that part out loud? I don't think so … which means he really can read me.

"Look, kid, think of her like the Pioneer Woman of Alabama, except with Christmas cookies."

"Alabama?" From what I've heard, the state has little more to offer than entertaining football games.

He nods at my puffy coat zipped to my neck. "You won't have to worry about any subzero temps there." Arnie waggles his eyebrows and grins.

I narrow my gaze on his yellowish teeth and sigh. Regardless of fair weather, I need more convincing. "How's the pay?"

His questioning grin transforms into a smile. "Now, that's my girl." Arnie pulls a contract from his desk drawer.

I shake my head. He shouldn't assume I'll take it already. However, he has a track record of talking me into crazy projects. A decade ago, he had me directing commercials for personal injury lawyers and tampons. At the time, I was desperate for any experience, and though I hate to admit it, those lawyers paid well.

He promised it would all pay off one day. Sure enough, several years later, I could name my price with most any TV movie or after-school special. Now that I'm used to making money, I want to make a difference.

However, I also want a steady paycheck, which in this business means not waiting too long between jobs.

Not to mention that I've got my mom and a rescue cat to support. If I could ever convince Mom to stop ordering random odds and ends from infomercials, I might be able to take a longer break. Self-rolling garden hoses and spa-grade foot tubs won't pay for themselves. I still don't understand why she thought we needed a garden hose. We have two potted ferns on an apartment balcony.

"You okay, kiddo?"

I blink and focus on the offer Arnie put in front of me. "Yeah." I blink again. If I'm seeing this number correctly, I'm more than okay. Those network people sure know how to woo a person.

"How long is filming?"

"A week, maybe a few days more. They want to chronicle all the events and festivities that revolve around her holiday baking."

I blow out a puff of air and imagine the cliché ice skating

rinks and tree lightings. This may be my two worst nightmares rolled into one—reality TV Hallmark.

Arnie raises his eyebrows as if waiting on my response. "Unless, of course, you're reconsidering joining your mother on that singles' cruise to Cabo."

My stomach churns. This is the problem with having an agent so close to my family. He knows which buttons to push to make me commit to crazy jobs. He also knows I'd rather direct *and star* in a romance movie than join Mom on her holiday excursion.

Ever since I've been on my own, she's planned some sort of old people's outing over Christmas. I used to like that it freed me up to take an extra job. The irony is she continues to plan these trips even after moving in with me.

And people wonder why I'm not crazy about Christmas . . .

"So, what do ya say? Christmas in Dixie?"

Christmas in Dixie. That's not something you hear often. I stare out the icy window as snow peppers the streets. Then I glance down at my dirty boots, soiled with slush from walking here. "Do they have snow?"

Arnie grins. "Not a lick."

I take a deep breath and say something I'm sure I'll regret until the hefty paycheck clears. "Where do I sign?"

Earl Ed

"Attention customers, we will be closing in fifteen minutes." I turn off the speaker and sigh. Then I clear my throat loud enough for Liam to hear.

He ignores me, so I do it again. When he ignores me a second time, I holler, "Liam."

He jerks upright from slumping over the counter, where he was eye level to a high school girl's cleavage. His cheeks redden when he realizes I caught him ogling our customers—again. That's what happens when you hire your little cousin for holiday help as a favor to your aunt.

Liam doesn't want to be here no more than I want to meet with my parole officer. But we all do things to check off boxes, I suppose. Me to keep a free life. Liam to convince Aunt Robin he's actually a responsible adult. Good luck with that.

"Liam, I need you to make sure all the go-karts are in. The last round ends in five minutes."

"Okay." He lifts his chin, then winks at the girl before heading out the door.

"Ma'am, do you need anything?"

The girl smacks her gum and shrugs. "I'm just looking over prizes."

I notice the tickets in her hand from our arcade games. "How many you got?"

She purses her red lips and re-counts a long string of tickets. "One seventy-one."

I stare through the glass, now smeared with Liam's pheromones. I'll make him clean that while I meet with Bradley. "Looks like candy or fake tattoos."

She nods. "What kinda tats you got?"

I open the back of the glass and pull out a small box of fake tattoos. She picks a pink leopard-print butterfly, which doesn't surprise me at all. I pegged her as the type to get a Lisa Frank tramp stamp. Maybe after trying out this fake one for a week, she'll change her mind on the real thing.

She thanks me as I slide it across the counter. A sense of

accomplishment bubbles in me, as if I indirectly saved someone from making a stupid mistake.

Speaking of stupid mistakes, Bradley enters. We're cordial enough for me to call him an acquaintance—and occasionally a friend. Still, these quarterly meetings remind me of my stupidest mistake.

No, I'm not sporting a tramp stamp. More like a permanent stamp on my personal record.

Bradley tips that stupid tan cowboy hat at the remaining customers making their way toward the door.

"Y'all have a nice night," I call as they pass.

Once the last one leaves, he steps inside. "Earl Ed."

"Bradley." I glance at the door. "Do you mind changing that sign to "Closed"?

He flips the sign on the door before walking toward me. I circle around the counter and lead him to a booth by the snack bar. "I can make you up a milkshake or something if you want."

"I'm good." He slides to the edge of the booth and leans against the wall. "No need in dragging this out. Let's get to it." He clears his throat and taps the table. "Have you taken anything not yours? Have you been following the rules set for you?"

I shake my head.

Bradley leans forward. "What did you take?"

"Nothing." My voice is more defensive than I mean for it to be, but I'm frustrated by how these questions are better suited for a preschool teacher to ask a five-year-old. "I've been living by the letter."

Bradley nods. "I get it. These meetings seem pointless to me, too." He folds his hands on the table and stares at me. "Earl Ed, you're a good man. You have a good business. But that doesn't change the fact that you're on parole after stealing mail. Silly as it sounds, that's a federal offense."

"I know." I sigh and adjust my cap.

When I was nineteen, I thought I was ten feet and bulletproof. I knew the rules—laws—as a mail carrier. However, I didn't see how an occasional catalog or Netflix DVD could get me arrested. Besides, I always delivered the mail to the rightful recipient—just later than they wanted.

Then I got a little cocky and wasn't discreet. Like someone constantly breaking the speed limit, it eventually caught up with me.

Heavy footsteps stomp near the entrance, and Bradley and I turn to the door. Liam walks like he has a sack of taters on both shoulders.

"Aunt Carla called me. Said she's been texting you."

I roll my eyes, then pull my phone from my front overalls pocket. Several texts from my mom pop up. All them say some version of "where are you?"

I type "leaving work" and put the phone back in my pocket. "Bradley, I'm apparently late for family supper. You got any more questions?"

Bradley opens his clasped hands and wrinkles his mouth. "No. I know you've been keeping your nose clean and all—just following protocol and doing my job."

"Appreciate it." I slide out of the booth and walk to Liam. I open my mouth to ask him to lock up, then think better of it.

"Liam, let's all head on to supper." I hook a thumb toward the counter. "But tomorrow, I'm gonna need you to clean that glass."

"Okay." He answers without looking in the direction I pointed, which means I'll have to specify which glass again tomorrow. Otherwise, I'll catch him wiping down the front of the claw machines.

Bradley follows us to the door, and we leave together. I lock up behind us and drive toward the road where most of my family lives. I'm not surprised that Liam tails me since he lives on the same road. That is until he continues following me past his own home.

When I park in front of Daddy and Mama's, most of my family's vehicles are parked out front, including Liam's parents' and the 1970s-model Firebird Aunt Misty drives. It's the spitting image of that car off *Smokey and the Bandit*. Her newest husband bought it for her a few months back.

Liam parks his truck beside mine, and Bradley drives up soon as we get out. He drops in on my family a lot. I figured that might end after my cousin he was sweet on got married this summer, but no. It's only gotten worse, since he swears he's in good with her husband now.

We walk between two rows of decorative lights that play Christmas music when our feet hit the sidewalk. The music ends once we make it on the porch. Mama must have it on motion-sensor mode.

I open the door to my cousin Michael's wife, Krystal, holding their one-year-old daughter. Who appears to be eating her own supper . . . from Krystal.

My face heats up with embarrassment for us and her, and maybe even the baby. "Whoa, Krystal. Put those puppies back in the pen."

"Sorry. She likes when I walk around while she eats." Krystal blushes and ducks into the theater room off the hallway.

Liam cranes his neck to watch her, and I slap the back of his head.

"What?" He rubs his head and scowls.

I catch Bradley peeking out of the corner of his eye, too. Deciding it's not a good idea to slap my parole officer, I march toward the kitchen. "Come on, we're already late."

I count about four Christmas trees before we reach the kitchen entrance. Every year, Mama adds more. It's like she's in competition with Aunt Robin for who can stuff the most trees in their house. Aunt Robin drives some stiff competition, considering her house is half the size of ours.

Not that her house is small. Ours is just, well, excessive.

The kitchen island is filled with Mama's fancy cookies. Fat Santa heads smile up at me as I approach the table. Liam and Bradley join me a minute later, both holding a cookie.

Mama glances at Bradley and presses her lips together. "Some of us may have to eat in the dining room." That's her Southern belle way of saying, "I didn't plan on this many people coming."

She plasters on a smile and continues. "First I have an announcement to make now that everyone's here." She slants her eyes at Daddy, who stops unrolling his napkin. Why Mama bothers to use cloth napkins and real silverware with this bunch is beyond me.

"What did Carla say?" G-Paw yells in G-Maw's face.

She flinches, then reaches over and adjusts his hearing aid until it squeaks. "She's got something to tell us!" I'm certain people on the other end of the county heard her. What's important, though, is that G-Paw did. He nods and smiles.

G-Maw winks at Mama, signaling her to continue. Mama smiles at her, then at the rest of us. Her face lights up like the outside Christmas lights shining through the patio doors.

"I've known about this for some time, but got the news today that it's official."

"You're pregnant!" Aunt Misty claps enthusiastically.

A few people roll their eyes, and Daddy scowls at his sister, who is the only one dumb enough to assume my mom could still get pregnant. Then again, Misty has her own toddler.

Instead of dignifying Misty with a response, Mama continues. "I have been selected by a major network to have my own baking show!" She clasps her hands, then holds them under her chin.

My family is a mixed bag of cheering, asking questions, and staring at the food. I zero in on Daddy to get his reaction. I can't tell if he's excited or aggravated about the show, but I can tell he's hungry. With a fork in one hand and a knife in the other, his eyes are locked on the turkey in front of him.

"Will you get to go to New York?" Aunt Robin asks. I vaguely recall Mama mentioning New York, as I was more interested in my family's reactions than her speech.

"No." Mama wavers her head. "I mean, maybe I could go to the studio sometime."

Robin clasps her hands together. "That would be great. We could make it a girls' trip with Carly and Lacie."

"Don't forget me," Aunt Misty mumbles around a mouthful of potato salad. Nobody answers her except G-Maw, who scolds her for eating before the blessing.

"They are coming here to film, at our house."

Daddy drops his silverware on his plate, and everyone turns toward the clanking noise. With all eyes on him, he has no choice but to say something. "Here, at the house?"

Mama nods, then her smile expands to take over the whole lower half of her face.

Daddy shakes his head. "Carla, you know how I feel about Northerners in the house."

She grips his hand, which is still resting on the edge of his plate where he dropped his fork. "Earl, honey, these are professionals. They're not going to try and steal your guns."

"You said you had buns?" G-Paw yells.

G-Maw talks to his ear. "We'll pass the bread in a minute." She grins, then shrugs at the rest of us when he seems satisfied with her answer. Sometimes it's best to just go with what he thinks we said.

"Can we eat now?" Daddy's forehead wrinkles as he gives Mama his sternest face.

"Yes, dear. Would you like to bless the food?"

The word "food" has barely left her lips when Daddy starts reciting the shortest prayer I've ever heard him pray. No mention of thanks for liberties and gun rights and crops and such. Just thanks for the food. He must really be hungry.

Immediately after his "amen," he forks a large helping of the sliced turkey piled in front of him. Everyone passes around plates, filling them high with meat and vegetables. G-Paw's thin lips turn up when Carly plunks a dinner roll on his plate.

Mama answers more questions about the show and filming dates. Daddy comments that at least he will be at work while they're here. She ignores that comment and continues discussing with Robin and Carly which cookies she should showcase.

"Let's talk about what's really important," Misty butts in with a mouthful of okra. "What should I wear for the first filming?" She smooths a piece of bleached blond hair out of her face. "This could be my big break."

G-Maw purses her lips. "I'm sure you'd break a leg." Her voice is clipped and sarcastic. Daddy lets out a deep belly laugh.

I can't wait until I'm old enough to say what I think and laugh at everything with no consequences. I'm currently at the age where people are starting to call me "sir," but I still have to mind my manners.

"Earl Ed, I'll need your help getting the director from the airport, if you don't mind."

I start to ask why a highfalutin production company can't get him a rental car, but I clamp my mouth shut and nod. Despite all I've been through, my mama has never treated me like less than. She visited me religiously when I was in jail and never shamed me. That's more than I can say for Daddy.

Krystal walks in the room with Colleen. I shade my eyes when she passes just in case she's got something out of place. The conversation continues and Krystal asks what everyone is talking about. Mama gets her up to speed.

I fork potatoes as Mama's smile grows with every detail. I absolutely don't want to drive to the airport to pick up some city-slicker director, but I can't say no to Mama.

CHAPTER TWO

Earl Ed

The last thing I wanted to do today was drive to Atlanta. I grip my steering wheel and curse the traffic around me. Even worse, I had to leave my seventeen-year-old sister in charge of Double Drive. That's the problem with my only employees being young and part time. However, I'd pick her over Liam anytime.

My truck idles as I creep over a bridge filled with semi-trucks and Teslas. My bright blue Dodge sticks out like a sore thumb, which is what that hitchhiker will soon have if he doesn't lower his sign and quit staring in my window. Of all the people to stop beside, I swear.

At last, the light ahead turns green and I put my truck in gear. Two massive poodles bark at me from a convertible as I pass. The airport exit comes into view, and my nerves unbuckle the slightest bit.

When Mama said I needed to go to the airport, I

assumed she meant Birmingham. At least she packed me a Tupperware of cookies for the ride.

I cram a chocolate-covered snowman in my piehole and flip my blinker in preparation of turning. The guy beside me apparently didn't see the blinker because he flips something else. I shove another snowman in my mouth and fight the urge to honk.

Two more cookies ease my temper enough to make it to the airport without any casualties. Unfortunately, that sets me back several calories.

For the last few months, I've tried to cut back. As a kid, I was "Michael's chubby cousin." Our mamas quit making us match for Easter Sunday when they couldn't find the same shirts for me in the husky section. In high school, all the girls wanted to be my friend, but never nothing more. The only place my size brought praise was on the football field.

Maybe it's turning thirty or needing more energy to run a business verses rotting away in a jail cell, but I decided it's time to drop a few.

I double-check Mama's text to make sure I'm in the right location before finding a park. Wait . . .

I told Mack to look for a sign with his name.

Oh shoot. I didn't make a sign. Why couldn't she say something like "look for the heavyset guy in overalls," which is my adult equivalent to "Michael's chubby cousin." I wipe sweat from my brow. *Think, Earl Ed.*

I park the truck and climb out. Sign, sign. Where's my sign?

A preverbal light goes off above my head as I spot a box of motor oil in the bed of my truck. I pull out my pocket knife and cut one of the box flaps. Hmm . . . best leave that knife in the truck. I shove it in my console and dig for a pen.

Five minutes later, the inside of my truck is ramshackle and I've found nothing to write with besides the knife and a can of orange spray paint I use to mark paintball targets.

I opt for the paint and spray "Mack Magee" across the cardboard. There, Mack. Here's your sign. Then I lock everything up and head for the doors.

Inside, the airport is everything I feared it would be—big, busy, and overwhelming. I haven't ventured anywhere past Mississippi since my parole kicked in, and even the coolest casinos in Tunica couldn't compare to this rat race.

My eyes scan the area for the pickup spot, and my face and neck start to sweat as I take in all the sights and sounds. Funny how a crowd this large can make me nervous. Aside from the parades and high school football games in Apple Cart, I haven't been immersed in this much society in a long time. And those crowds wouldn't amount to a tenth of the people here.

I close my eyes for a second and force myself to chill. Then I continue toward the signs leading in the direction of my gate. People jump on a moving walkway like at the casinos. Before I have time to think, I hop on one, too.

I hold my sign with both hands so the paint can dry without dripping. The belt comes to an end, and I hobble onto steady ground. Even with losing some weight, I'm still not the most agile.

The herd migrates toward the baggage claim area, and I follow again. I stand between a woman with giant balloons and a rich-looking man in a suit, then hold up Mack's sign. I've never met a director, but imagine him tall and thin, with some sort of modernist goatee. Maybe a scarf around his neck and a pair of skinny jeans.

My nerves start to uncoil now that I'm no longer shuffling among hundreds of strangers. I hang back with my cardboard sign better fit for someone soliciting a handout than picking up a media person.

That's why people like me stay out of Atlanta.

A few people head my way, including a tall, young guy who I'm certain is Mack. Then he walks off with the guy in the expensive suit. I rock back on my heels and scan the people picking up luggage. Maybe Mack is older or even short or even . . .

"You must be my driver."

I drop my eyes to the voice beside me. A female voice, coming from a female face. A very pretty female face. One with thick lips and wide, brown eyes. I'm so caught off guard that I drop the sign. When I bend to pick it up, so does she. Our hands touch, and my fingers flare. I pull back, not wanting to give off creeper vibes.

Since I'm a bigger dude who's done some jail time, I'm always leery of creeping out good-looking women.

She picks up the sign, and we stand slowly. Then she hands it to me and half smiles. I take it, making sure not to touch her hand this time. My nerves can't take it again. The combination of airport anxiety and withdrawals from not dating in a decade has me on edge.

"I'm Mackenzie Magee, but my agent calls me Mack."

I stare at the small hand shoved in front of my chest like it's a sacred object I'm not supposed to touch. When she narrows her eyes, I shake her hand. She has a firm grip for a such a little thing, especially for a Northerner.

After I release her hand, I grab the two bags beside her. We start walking toward the exit when she asks, "And you are?"

"Oh, sorry. I'm Earl Ed Mayberry, Carla's son."

She nods. "Earl Ed. Huh, I've never heard that name

before." She wavers her head. "I mean, of course, I've heard of Earl and Ed, just never together like that."

"Family name." I stop and wipe a row of sweat from my brow, then continue pulling the suitcases.

"Is it always this hot down here?"

"Pretty much." Although I'm sure she's the reason for me sweating in December.

We walk in silence until we reach the truck. I toss the cardboard sign in the bed, then open the back door for her bags. I Uber enough to know people don't care to have their luggage rolling around the bed of my truck. Then I rush around and open her door before she can.

"Oh, well, thanks." She blinks, a shocked expression on her face.

Maybe I overdid the Southern hospitality. I get in and resort to nervous small talk in an effort to play it cool. "So, you ever been to Bama?"

"No." She shakes her head and pulls a pair of wide-rimmed sunglasses from this tiny backpack. "I've been to Florida a few times and Texas once or twice, but mainly stay north." She slides the glasses up the bridge of her nose.

"I don't travel much. Today's the first time I've been to Atlanta since a Braves game a few years back."

Mackenzie turns to me, her mouth parting. "Really?"

"Yeah, I'm not one to stray far." Of course, it's hard to when you're either in jail or having to check in with Bradley before you can travel so many miles.

She laughs. My stomach churns. Is it *that* funny that I stay close to home?

"I saw the funniest sign at TSA."

Good, so it's not me. For a minute, I was worried those cookies might make a second appearance. "What's that?"

"No weapons, contraband, or taxidermy."

Now it's my turn to laugh. "Actually, that's a funny story."

I proceed to tell Mack all about my friend Jack and how he rolled a fully mounted deer into the Atlanta airport to chase down the woman who's now his wife. Either she'll find it amusing or want to tuck tail and run back to New York, but it gives me something to talk about on the ride to Apple Cart.

Mackenzie

It's one thing to read a sign that states, "No weapons, contraband or taxidermy." However, I never expected Earl Ed would know the story behind how taxidermy made the cut, much less know the guy who brought the deer into the Atlanta airport.

With every detail of the story, I ask myself what was so wrong with another holiday season in Canada. Sure, it's freaking freezing up there. But they don't have issues with people rolling around stuffed moose.

I study the sights as we pass through Apple Cart, Alabama. Earl Ed explained that the Jack guy lives there. Earl Ed's family lives in Wisteria, which is on the other end of the county. As we venture farther from any civilization, I'm afraid this Wisteria is on the wrong side of the tracks, as they say.

"The production company got me a room at the Quality Inn."

Earl Ed stares at me like I've grown another head. "You serious?"

"Yeah, is there someplace better people stay?"

"Most stay with friends or kinfolk. I guess if you ain't got any here, that's an option, but it's kinda a dump. There's always Gamer's Paradise."

"Where the deer guy lives?"

"Yeah. I think he's got a full lodge right now, but I might can call and see if they got a spare room."

So my options are a dump or a deer lodge. I sigh. "I guess let's check out Quality Inn before we make any decisions." I stare out my window at nothing but fields and a Waffle House, debating if I should rent an RV.

"I can take you there, but if you don't like it, just let me know."

I nod. A few minutes later, we pass a large arch with "Double Drive" painted across it. Then Earl Ed puts on his blinker. We turn into the parking lot for Quality Inn. It consists of six rooms, at least that are visible from the front, and has what appears to be a liquor store and Mexican restaurant in the same building. The signs read: Quality Inn, The Hole, Enchilada. *Strange.* Something tells me this place rents more rooms by the hour than night.

Earl Ed parks his massive truck in front of the door marked "Office." He glances at me, then his eyebrows pull down as he frowns. "I'll get your bags."

I practically jump from his truck, which easily wins the contest for tallest Uber vehicle I've taken. He retrieves my bags and follows me to the door. Then he opens it before I can again. This guy is working hard for a tip.

A weird buzzer sound dings when we enter. A thin, older guy with an eye patch welcomes us in a raspy voice. The kind of voice that comes from either having laryngitis or smoking half his life.

"Welcome to Quality Inn. Can I help you?"

I unbuckle my purse and pull out my ID. "I have a reservation for Mackenzie Magee."

He opens a large calendar book, then puts on a pair of glasses and squints his one good eye at the page. "Ah, got ya right here, darlin'."

Earl Ed takes a step closer to me, and my shoulders relax a little knowing he's here in case the skinny pirate man tries something sketchy.

Pirate man hands me a key with the number four on the keychain. I take it and hold my breath. Lord only knows who else has had this key—and this room.

As we turn to walk out, Earl Ed asks, "What happened to your eye?"

I freeze, and my entire body numbs. You can't just ask someone what happened to their eye! He could've been born without an eyeball or had some kind of vision cancer.

"Got in a scuffle at Enchilada the other night."

Earl Ed nods, and his nostrils flare. He steps outside with my bags, and drags me along with him. When we're at room four, he sighs heavily behind me. "I can't let you stay here, Mackenzie."

I snicker. "I'm from Jersey and grew up poor. Trust me, I've seen a lot."

He shakes his head. "This is no place for a lady."

My face flushes at the sincere concern in his eyes. Wow, his eyes are super blue, especially against the old brick building and asphalt parking lot.

"You're sweet, but I think I can—" I shove open the door and a huge rat runs out.

I scream and jump into Earl Ed's arms. He holds me against him and slams the door shut. I ball up against his chest until I catch my breath. When I blink up at him, he smiles.

"Now can I find you someplace better?"

I nod, then open my mouth to say he can put me down. Before the words come out, he walks me back to his truck and sets me inside. Then he gets my bags and gently places them in the back.

"Hand me the key."

I hold out the key in my fingertips like I'm holding the rat by the tail.

He takes it. "Hang tight. I'll be back."

I sit in silence after he closes the door and goes in the motel office. The "Quality" part of the light-up sign fizzles in and out as I stare ahead.

A few seconds later, Earl Ed gets in the truck and pulls a phone from his front overalls pocket. He texts something, then waits, then texts again.

After reading a final text, he strokes his short beard and sighs. "That was Jack. He's hosting a Civil War Reenactment retreat this week. No vacancy, just like with Baby Jesus."

I scrunch my forehead, confused at what a war reenactment has to do with Jesus.

Earl Ed slaps his steering wheel, causing me to flinch. "That's it. I'm taking you to stay with my parents. They have plenty of room."

"Whoa, wait."

"Don't worry, it's a nice, clean place."

My stomach buckles. I didn't mean to offend him. "No, I know that. I mean, come on, we're here to film your mom cook." I laugh nervously, then regret insinuating that her house wouldn't be clean if we weren't filming. "What I mean is I can't legally stay on-site at the filming location, especially since it's her home."

"Oh." He strokes his beard again and taps the steering wheel with his thumb before facing me. "What about my place?"

"Your place?" My shoulders tense again. I can't expect the

21

guy to cart me around all week and give me a place to stay, too. Can I? He is good with shutting down rat holes and guys who get in bar fights. Or Mexican restaurant fights, to be exact. Though I'm sure that liquor store played a role in him needing an eye patch.

"Yeah, it's right across the county line."

I keep silent. Aside from dressing like the men on *Little House on the Prairie*, Earl Ed seems like a standup guy. He's polite, keeps an immaculate truck, drives well, and makes pleasant conversation. Of course, he did welcome me with cardboard, but nobody's perfect.

Less than a minute later, he turns off the road and drives under the Double Drive arch. We pull up to a clubhouse of sorts with a go-kart track behind it. Behind that is a mini-golf course decorated with Christmas lights. A large blowup Grinch waves when we get out.

"So . . . You live at a mini-golf course?"

He laughs. "Yes and no." He takes my bags from the back and meets me in front of the truck. "This is my business." He points to the top of the clubhouse. "Upstairs is my loft apartment."

I lift my chin. Living in New York, I'm well acquainted with lofts above businesses. "Neat."

"Now, it's still a work in progress, but it's got plenty of room, and it's clean and warm. No rats, roaches, or eye patches."

I laugh, and he joins me. His face lights up, and I see a hint of dimples popping beneath his facial hair. He smiles, then continues toward the building with my bags.

We climb a small porch and enter a room filled with game consoles. "Now, I haven't added a way in from outside yet, so you have to enter through the back hallway."

I follow him through the building, past a counter with tons of stuffed animals behind it, then a café area with booths and fountain drinks. He leads me past the café counter to a hallway, then opens a door to a staircase.

Earl Ed lifts my bags and climbs the stairs like a pro. That's no easy feat since I packed several heavy pairs of shoes. He opens another door at the top of the staircase to reveal a large room with hardwood floors.

My mouth drops as I gaze around. It's definitely a man's place, with all leather furniture and little decor. Nothing more than a few fish and deer heads mounted on the wall. Oh, and a massive TV in the corner.

"I have two bedrooms and a bathroom. The kitchen isn't done yet, so I'm afraid you'll have to use the commercial one downstairs."

I stroll through the living area and notice what will be the kitchen. It's nothing more than walls, wiring, and an island that isn't finished. "This is great. No worries about the kitchen. We'll have some sort of craft services."

"Crafts? I guess there's room for them in the spare bedroom."

I laugh. "No, craft services. It's the food provided by the production."

He wrinkles his forehead and shrugs. "All right. But you're welcome to my kitchen anytime, and I cook regularly."

"Thanks." A calmness washes over me when he opens the door to the spare bedroom.

There's a simple dresser and queen-size bed. It's airy and simple, yet comforting.

"Sorry I haven't given much attention to furnishing the place. Nobody goes in this room much. It probably wouldn't even have a bed had my daddy's sister's husband's ex-wife's brother not needed a place to stay when he came through town to drop off some chihuahuas."

I try and follow that train of thought, but can't. Instead, I plop down on the edge of the bed.

Earl Ed parks my bags by the door. "The bathroom is across from this room, and there's a washer and dryer in that closet." He hooks his thumb over his shoulder toward the hallway. "My room is at the end of the hall if you need anything. Oh, and if you're hungry, I can cook you some supper."

I widen my eyes. I didn't expect such hospitality from my Uber driver. "Well, if you're offering, a grilled cheese would be nice."

"Done."

Before I can thank him, Earl Ed disappears down the hall. I hear footsteps going downstairs as he heads toward a working kitchen to prepare my grilled cheese. That's about all I can stomach after a full day of flights and seeing a rat up close, not to mention an eye patch.

I lay my head back and close my eyes to rest until my food is ready. I've heard a lot of strange things about Alabama, and I'm certain I will hear—and see—more before this filming wraps.

CHAPTER THREE

Earl Ed

I whistle to myself as I flip bacon and check on my biscuits. School lets out today, which means we'll either be really busy or really dead, depending on how many people go out of town. Most people stay home for Christmas around here, but some travel beforehand or on New Year's.

My phone pings for the fifth time since I woke up. I check it and shake my head. Mama won't leave well enough alone. Speaking of well enough, Mackenzie steps in the doorway.

"Good morning." I smile and wave the tongs in my hand before flipping more bacon. The oven goes off, and I retrieve the biscuits.

She enters the kitchen and leans against the counter. "Wow, you really can cook."

"You mean the grilled cheese last night didn't tip you off?"

She snickers at my sarcasm.

I pull a pan of eggs from the microwave where I left them to keep warm, then put the biscuits on a plate. As I'm draining the bacon grease, my text sound pings again.

I grab my phone and type in a quick reply to let her know we'll be there shortly. Then I nod at the food. "Help yourself. Mama's been on me to bring you by. I told her you're still getting ready to buy you some time."

She smiles as I hand her a plate. I turn my phone on silent and shove it in my jeans pocket before fixing my own plate.

"Sorry there's not a table upstairs yet. We can eat on the couches, or here in a booth."

"That's fine." Mackenzie takes her plate to the dining area and slides into a corner booth.

I catch a whiff of her perfume or body spray when she passes me. Whatever the scent, it smells better than anything in here. Well, except for the bacon.

I grab two forks and a pitcher of tea, then join her. "I usually drink sweet tea or water, but we have milk, juice." I tilt my head toward the drink fountain. "And Pepsi products."

"Water's fine."

I take some cups from the counter and fix her ice water, then fill a cup of ice for my tea. Mackenzie moans loudly behind me. I'm so startled I almost spill my ice.

When I turn around, she's chomping on a biscuit. I slide her drink in front of her as she swallows.

"This is the best biscuit I've ever eaten. Where did you learn to cook?"

"Prison." My entire body tingles when I realize what I said. Usually, it isn't a big deal because I'm so used to everyone knowing.

She bursts out laughing. "Good one."

I grin nervously. Best let her think that's a joke. I doubt she'd want to stay with an ex-convict. And since we're running out of housing options, she may have to find a stable like Baby Jesus.

Mackenzie shares a little about some of her previous projects while we finish eating. She has a lot of movies in her past, though none I've seen.

"I'm pretty sure my mama and aunt have seen some of your work. They watch that stuff all the time." I down the rest of my tea, savoring every last drop. I limit my sweet tea consumption nowadays, so every ounce is like liquid gold.

She points a fork toward me and winks. "And that's why I'm ready for a change. All those movies are the same story told by a different person about a different couple."

I shrug. "Can't say I've seen any. I'm more of an Adam Sandler fan myself."

Mackenzie laughs. "Sandler's surprised me with some of his later work, I'll give him that."

I turn my cup up to catch some of the ice, then chew as I check the time on the wall clock behind the counter. "If you're ready, I can take you to meet my mother before I open for the day."

"No, you're busy. I'll just get an Uber."

I say nothing and wait patiently while she takes out her phone and opens the app.

Her forehead creases as she reads the results. "Earl Ed Mayberry . . . and it looks like you're already here." She raises an eyebrow.

"Yeah, I'm kinda the only one around."

"Fine by me." She crinkles her mouth in a flirty way. At least, in what I imagine is a flirty way. "Let me grab my purse."

I watch her retreat upstairs, then clear our table. I'm in

the kitchen washing the egg pan when Mackenzie slides beside me and rolls up her sleeves.

"Let me help you."

"Nah, I've got this, and you're a guest."

She lifts one corner of her mouth. "Yeah, but you cooked all this, cooked last night, gave me a good room to stay in."

I smile. She's not at all like I thought she'd be. Partly because I'd assumed most big-wig, big-city people were rude. And I also expected a dude, not some cute chick who can barely climb in my truck.

"I insist," she says.

Realizing I've been grinning like a possum at her for an awkward moment, I hand her a dish towel. "You can dry."

I swallow and stare at the dishes until all are clean. Then I dry my hands and wait as she dries hers.

We walk in silence to my truck. I open her door and help her inside.

"Thank you. This has got to be the tallest vehicle I've ever ridden in."

I laugh. "Six-inch lift kit."

She scrunches her nose as if she doesn't understand. I get in and back out of the parking lot.

"When do you guys start filming?" Maybe making small talk will lower my heart rate. It spiked when I helped her into my truck.

"Tomorrow morning. The crew is mainly coming from Birmingham, but local-ish."

"I wondered why you didn't bring a crew."

She snickers. "I don't have my own crew. I work with whomever the production hires for the job. They're usually local to the project."

I nod. None of this makes sense to me. She explains a lot of the jobs involved in filming a movie or even a commercial. It all sounds a little over the top, especially to video my mom make cookies. I could do that with my phone. Heck, I have done that with my phone for her Instagram account.

The pine trees thin as we drive onto my parents' land. Christmas lights flank every shrub on the way. I stop in the center of the front circle drive.

"Wow." Mackenzie's mouth drops. "This is where you grew up?"

"Yeah." I climb out and palm the back of my neck as I wait for her to climb down.

She scans the front of the house, her mouth dropping another notch every few seconds. "I had no idea there were houses like this out here." She raises her hands and shakes them my way. "No offense, just Apple Cart County seems so . . ."

"Redneck?"

She shrugs. "I was going more for simple, but I guess that could work."

"There's rich rednecks, too."

"Apparently." Mackenzie steps toward the fountain, and Christmas music comes on. It continues playing in sync with where she's walking. She laughs and walks back and forth.

I chuckle. It's fun watching her dictate the song. She's made it halfway through "We Wish You a Merry Christmas" when the front door flies open.

"Earl Ed, there you are." Mama rushes down the front porch steps wearing one of her Christmas aprons. She and Aunt Robin are obsessed with them.

She stops in front of me, then jerks her head toward Mackenzie. Mama's eyes widen, and she picks up a strand of Mackenzie's wavy hair. "You're so adorable!" Before I can stop her, she wraps Mackenzie in a hug and starts swaying. "Welcome to our home."

I tug Mama's shoulder, pulling her off Mackenzie. She's

friendly to a fault, which isn't everyone's cup of tea. "Mama, this—"

She slaps my arm and cuts me off. "You didn't tell me you were bringing a girl by. She's beautiful. A little thin maybe, but nothing my cooking can't fix."

"No, Mama."

"Oh, don't be so bashful, Earl Ed. If anyone deserves happiness, it's you."

I swipe my hand down my face. This is getting out of hand. Mama never listens. I glance at Mackenzie, who's smirking as if she's trying desperately to hold back a laugh.

"See, I told you once you lost a little weight and got out of jail, things would turn around."

My mouth goes dry. I couldn't shut her up now if I tried. I turn to Mackenzie, whose face has gone pale.

Just great. Five minutes into meeting my mother, and Mackenzie has learned I'm a fat felon.

Mackenzie

So the part about learning to cook in prison wasn't a joke. However, I'm not one to judge people based on their past, and he didn't murder me in my sleep last night.

Besides, I'd risk sleeping down the hall from Earl Ed any day over staying at the Quality Inn beside the liquor store and eye-patch pirate.

Carla goes on about how Earl Ed deserves happiness, and I get the urge to save him. Pay him one back for rescuing me from the rat motel.

I stick my hand between them. "I'm Mack Magee, your director."

Carla's jaw drops, and she freezes for a minute before shaking my hand. "Oh dear, I'm so sorry." She drops my hand and covers her forehead. "What a terrible mistake."

I smile. "It's fine, really. I'm Mackenzie, but my agent always refers to me as Mack." As much as I hate to embarrass Carla, I had to intervene. Poor Earl Ed.

Carla pats him on the shoulder. "Sorry, son." Then she turns to me. "But you are adorable." She loops an arm through mine and walks me toward the porch.

"The Little Drummer Boy" plays as we pass by walkway lights. If I have to hear Christmas music, synchronized to motion lights is the way to go.

She opens the massive wooden door and leads me inside. More Christmas lights reflect on marble flooring, and almost outshine the massive chandelier overhead. I count maybe five trees on our way down the hall. A few more trees flock the corners of the kitchen, and I contemplate how we can work around them for filming.

Footsteps come behind us, and I turn to find Earl Ed standing in the entry. Carla lets go of my arm and motions to her son. "Earl Ed, be a dear and bring that platter over here, please."

She pulls a pair of reading glasses and a notebook from a built-in desk, then waves me toward the massive table. "Sit, relax. I'll show you what I do so you can better plan."

I slide back a chair, which is even heavier than it looks, but comfier than most couches. Everything in the room is sleek and luxurious, from the stainless-steel appliances to the vaulted ceiling, to this chair. If it weren't for framed Bible verses on the wall and goats wandering in the backyard, I'd think this was a Kardashian home.

I watch the goats as Carla thumbs through her notebook. They're tiny and rambunctious. "Are your goats babies?"

Carla fans a hand. "Oh, we don't have any . . ." She pauses. Her eyes widen as she peers over my head, then stands. "Earl Ed, can you get G-Maw's goats out of the yard? They're gonna eat my decorations."

"Yes, ma'am." Earl Ed smirks at me before setting two large trays of cookies on the table and retreating out the patio door.

I stare at the cookies. They're so precise and uniform that it's hard to believe they're homemade. She also put a lot of detail into the frosting. From the cowboy Santa to the camouflage snowman, it's evident why the network would want to feature Carla. I've never seen anything like them. My eye gravitates toward a deer in a Christmas sweater, with ornaments on its antlers. Such minute detail, down to the snowflakes on the sweater. I think this one's my favorite.

Carla sits down and adjusts her glasses. "You like the deer?"

I nod. "It's eccentric, but in a good way."

She pushes the plate in front of me. "Taste it."

Literal visions of sugar plums dance in my head as I relive my dessert PTSD from all the Christmas movies. However, working in this industry has taught me to always keep the talent happy. And growing up poor with a flighty mom has taught me to never turn down free home cooking—sweets included.

I pick up the cookie and bite into the antler. Hints of cinnamon and nutmeg hit my tongue, and I sigh audibly for the second time today—both while eating. Even if Earl Ed perfected his skills in prison, he no doubt inherited raw talent from his mom.

"What do you think?"

I lick the corner of my mouth and swallow. "Wow, that's

so good." I turn the cookie in my hand, examining the inside. How is it crumbly and moist at the same time? She must be some sort of good witch.

"Thanks, that's one of my favorite flavors. I feel like the nutmeg really brings out what you'd expect a deer to taste like." Carla giggles. "If a deer were sweet, of course." Her face goes serious. "Real deer tastes nothing like nutmeg."

I nod, unsure of whether I've ever tasted actual deer. If so, it would be from ordering a mystery meat sandwich at that food truck near Arnie's office.

Carla turns the notebook so I'm facing her writing. "Here are all the events and usual gatherings in Apple Cart County this month."

To not sound like a broken record, I think "wow" rather than say it. But with parades and church functions and dinners and whatever Angel Tree is, her social calendar already resembles a production schedule. This community is quite the hopping place.

"You bake cookies for all these events?"

She nods. "And for some friends and their family events as well."

I bite off the deer's other antler and peek out the window. Earl Ed walks by with a baby goat under his arm. When Carla starts to turn that way, I talk to get her attention. I'm sure he doesn't need any distraction while wrangling goats.

"Your kitchen is lovely. We should have plenty of room to work in here."

"Thank you. Y'all are welcome to film anywhere in the house. I finished decorating the theater room yesterday."

My eyes widen. "Theater room?"

She nods. "It's always the last on my list since I only do simple red and green lighting around the crown molding."

By the nonchalantness in her voice, you'd think she were talking about something more common, like a family room.

Maybe lots of families have home theaters—just none I've ever met. Well, except for a few actors.

"How do I need to wear my hair for the show?" Carla smooths her shoulder-length gray hair back.

I smile. She's very attractive, so I'm certain hair and makeup will appreciate an easy client. "We'll have someone to do all that, and to help pick out your wardrobe." My eyes fall to her waist. "Though I'm sure they will love that Christmas apron."

She runs a hand down the cartoon gingerbread people spread across her lap and smiles. "Thanks. My sister-in-law and I picked this up at the flea market last year."

I find it oddly refreshing that she shops at a flea market. Although judging from her home, the bargain shopping stops at clothes—possibly even aprons.

We chat about how she started baking cookies as a hobby, which morphed into a side business, then her main business. She gives away almost as much as she sells, especially this time of year. Even with baking for every occasion, Christmas is still her favorite.

A slight bitterness rises in me when she goes on about all the family traditions and teaching her daughter and Earl Ed to bake cookies for Santa. If we were home on Christmas Eve, my mother would tell me to leave Santa a Snickers and one of her Weight Watcher shakes. I guess she didn't want to bother with making anything, and it made sense to put out something she planned on eating anyway.

Now I'm a jaded woman in her early thirties caught in a trap of directing magical Christmas movies. I argued that nobody lived like those scripts with happy family gatherings and Christmas carols. But if anyone does, it's got to be Carla Mayberry.

CHAPTER FOUR

Earl Ed

I twist the next bulb and pray it's the dud. Nope. I may as well go ahead and change out this whole blasted string of lights. I suddenly sympathize with Chevy Chase, and my golf course lights don't hold a candle to his house.

As I work on untwisting the lights from around a fake bull's horn, Mackenzie walks up.

"Hi."

"Hey." I straighten and roll up what I've untangled so far. "I didn't expect Mama to keep you this long."

I assumed she'd buzz me for a ride. I act casual, as if I have better things to do than be her chauffeur. Like unravel broken lights and chase down goats. Both of which are true.

"She didn't. The producer called and said the crew was coming in. One of them picked me up and drove me to their trailers."

"Where are they?" I glance around, not noticing anyone other than customers riding go-karts or golfing nearby.

"Quality Inn parking lot."

I shake my head. "Really?"

"Yeah, but a few of them will commute from Tuscaloosa. They said I could come stay with them."

"Oh." My face falls, and I'm no longer able to play it cool. I've only known the woman a day and a half, but what I know so far, I like. Still, it's not like I can wear her down by feeding her good food. Someone like her would never go for a fat felon like me.

"I told them I had a place already."

I lift my face to read her expression. There's no pity in her eyes. "You can stay with them if you need to—or want to."

A grin creeps across her lips. "If you don't mind, I was hoping I could just stay here."

"You want to stay here?" The shock is strong in that sentence. I bite my tongue to keep from saying something stupid.

"Of course I do. I have my own nice room, the food is great, and it's only a few miles from your parents' house."

I smile. "That's exactly what I said when I started my business."

She laughs. "I'll be glad to have the production company pay you what they planned on paying the motel."

"No, I can't accept that."

"Are you sure?"

I nod. "Absolutely. To be honest, I've enjoyed the company." My face heats up at admitting that, but it is true. Most of my buddies are coupled up or have moved away.

"It's settled, then. We're temporary roomies." She smiles and extends a hand.

I stare at it a second, then give it a firm shake. Before I release her hand, I hear a familiar cackle. *Paul.*

He struts our way with Ms. Dot on his arm. I drop Mackenzie's hand and start fumbling around with the lights.

"Howdy, Earl Ed." Paul points his lime-green golf club toward Mackenzie. "And who do we have here?"

"Mackenzie Magee." She shakes Paul's hand, then Ms. Dot's.

Paul introduces both of them as Ms. Dot grins.

"It's a pleasure to meet you both."

"What brings you to town?" he asks.

I raise an eyebrow at Mackenzie and study her face. Most people not from around here don't understand why our old people are so nosy.

Unfazed, she answers, "I'm here for work."

That would satisfy most people, but not the folks of Apple Cart County. Especially since people don't travel through here for work.

Paul looks her up and down, then grins. "You're that film director, ain't ya?"

Mackenzie swallows, and I enjoy focusing on her throat moving a little too much. I really need to get out more.

Before she can answer, Ms. Dot chimes in. "I'm so excited to see Carla on TV! Will y'all be filming in front of a live audience? Where can I buy a ticket?"

Paul interrupts with, "Do you by chance work with *American Pickers*? I think I've got some things those guys might like."

"Uh, Paul, it's been great catching up, but I need to get Mackenzie to work." I chuckle and ball up the lights in one arm. Then I put my other hand on Mackenzie's back and lead her off the course.

I try and ignore the warmth of her soft sweater beneath my calloused hand, including the way her small back cups beneath my palm. Instead, I focus on my mission: shield Mackenzie from Apple Cart busybodies. It's for her own good. All anyone over sixty around here cares about is matchmaking and celebrity sightings. That's what happens when you retire in a town with nothing better to do.

I'll usher her upstairs and bring by dinner later.

That plan lasts all of five minutes before we meet a small group of teenagers near the kitchen area. "I think that's her," one girl says. She points to Mackenzie, and they all start chattering.

I notice Paul pecking away on a cell phone from the window. The teenagers start to approach us, and I rush Mackenzie toward the back. We stop by my office near the stairwell. My sister is in there printing flyers for the New Year's Eve blacklight paintball bash.

"Carly, could you go up front for a bit and help Liam?"

"Sure."

"Oh, and announce that we're about to shut the go-carts down for maintenance until tonight."

"Sure."

"Thanks."

Carly stacks the papers in her hands, then sets them on my desk. She passes us on her way to the front.

"Sorry about that. I know a place you can hide until they clear out." I open the door that leads to the basement and motion for Mackenzie to go first.

I follow her downstairs. I could've taken her upstairs, but I don't want to chance people seeing her in the windows or realizing she's staying here. Someone is likely to stalk her on the off chance they might get on camera.

Mackenzie glances at the broken-down go-karts and oil-stained concrete.

I wipe dust from a chair and bring it to her. "In case you want a seat. We can go up as soon as my sister clears out the course. I didn't want everyone stalking you or knowing you're staying upstairs."

She half-smiles. "That's so thoughtful. Your sister seems nice, too."

"Yeah, most of my bunch is good people. We only have a few loose screws in the family."

She narrows her eyes, then grins. I'm not sure all of what we say translates to her vocabulary, but after she meets Aunt Misty, she'll get what I mean by that.

I sit on the floor beside her and let out a puff of air. "So, how'd it go with my mom?"

She smiles. "Well. She's lovely. A true Southern lady."

I chuckle. "That's one way to put it. Sorry about her attacking you with hugs."

Mackenzie shakes her head. "Don't worry about it. I prefer that to other greetings I've had from *talent*." She makes air quotes around the word "talent," and we both laugh.

"I bet."

She bites her lip and picks at her fingernails before giving me a serious stare. "When you mentioned prison . . ."

I sigh. "I wasn't joking."

She narrows her eyes.

"Technically, it was just county jail, but I got arrested and convicted at nineteen." I expect her to run or at least push her chair farther from me. Instead, she frowns and leans closer.

"For what?"

My heart speeds up from both her compassion and my shame. I stroke my beard and lower my head. "It's embarrassing."

"What? Did you break one of those obscure laws like walking with ice cream in your pocket on a Sunday?"

I laugh. "No. There's a law about that?"

She shrugs. "There's something about ice cream in a pocket somewhere. Google weird old laws. You'll see."

I laugh again. "No, I wish. I stole mail."

"Like checks?"

I shake my head.

"Amazon packages?"

I shake my head again.

Her eyes bug. "Prescription drugs?"

I hold up a hand to stop her. "Catalogs and DVDs."

"Really?" She wrinkles her nose.

I nod. "Told you it was embarrassing."

She giggles. "And that put you in jail?"

"It was a federal offense."

"I don't think people even get catalogs and DVDs in the mail anymore."

"Maybe I'm the reason why." I wiggle my eyebrows, and she laughs.

"Maybe so." Mackenzie shuffles in her chair and turns toward me. "Wait, so like any DVDs and catalogs?"

I drop my head and moan. "Ugh. This is embarrassing." I lift my head to face her, my cheeks hot with shame. "Mostly Adam Sandler movies."

She laughs. "Well, you said you were a fan."

I lick my lips and sigh. "And for the other . . . Victoria's Secret."

She laughs so hard that she falls off the folding chair. I catch her before she hits the concrete. She falls back in my lap, laughing more. "I'm so sorry, that's just the funniest thing I've heard in a while."

"I was nineteen."

Mackenzie bows over and laughs again. "That's even funnier."

I should be offended, but I'm too relieved she's not scared of me. I'm also a little turned on by her flailing in my lap, even if it's from laughing at my expense.

We laugh together until we're both almost out of breath. Then I hear footsteps.

Carly sticks her head in the room and raises one eyebrow. "Sorry to interrupt."

Without thinking, I place Mackenzie back on her chair.

Carly tucks some hair behind her ear. "Yeah, um, the coast is clear upstairs."

"Thanks," I mumble. I stand and help Mackenzie to her feet.

We follow Carly upstairs. I try to shake off what just happened, even if I'm not sure what it was.

Mackenzie

I wait in the back parking lot of Double Drive as the crew members climb out of their van. Earl Ed was kind enough to let us meet here, since Quality Inn doesn't come with a conference room of any kind like most hotels.

His face filled with concern when I'd said we planned on meeting either in the cameraman's motel room—after a thorough rat check—or in the back of Enchilada. I didn't like either option, but Earl Ed had even stronger reservations.

He quickly offered Double Drive after closing for our brainstorming sessions and crew meetings, since he has plenty of room and no rats. I said I could call around town for a meeting room, but he insisted out of convenience and lack of nosy townspeople.

So here we are.

"Does this place have a bathroom?" Ziggy, the cameraman, asks in a strained voice, holding his stomach.

"Yes, go to the front of the building. It's to the right after you enter the main area," I say.

Still clutching his stomach, he rushes toward the building. The rest of the guys linger around the parking lot. I open the basement door to let them inside.

Earl Ed has a long table set up with several folding chairs and two space heaters in the corners. About the time everyone settles into a chair, he comes downstairs.

"Hi." He raises a hand, then returns it to his pocket. "I'm Earl Ed, nice to have y'all."

Different crew members say their greetings. I go around the table introducing everyone, some of whom I just met. As with most crews, we have a ragtag team made up of freelancers.

Some of the guys know one another from working together before, since most came from the same area. One guy likes to brag that he shot a commercial with the Alabama and Auburn quarterbacks. He's mentioned it at least three times today, but nobody seems to care—especially me.

"If anyone's hungry, I can fire up the grill," Earl Ed offers.

"Thanks, but we've already eaten at that Mexican joint by the motel." Rambo adjusts his bandana and pats his belly.

I have no clue what his real name is since he introduced himself as Rambo. As long as he runs the boom mic smoothly, I'll call him anything he wants.

Earl Ed takes drink orders, and I follow him upstairs to help carry them.

Once we're at the drink dispenser, I say, "Thanks again for offering a room."

"No problem. It's a big, empty space used for nothing but go-kart parts. It may as well see some action."

My face flares up at the word "action," as my mind flashes back to me falling in his arms and laughing before his sister came down. For a split second, I thought he might try and kiss me. And for another split second, I thought I'd have let him.

Earl Ed is nothing like the guys I've dated. Not that I date that much. Most guys aren't into a woman who works all the time, then goes home to a high-maintenance mother and rescue cat.

On the rare occasion I do date, it's usually a guy working in my industry. Never anyone who does random tasks for his mother, or shows up to the airport with a spray-painted sign, or wears overalls. But also never someone so concerned with the well-being of others.

I start filling cups with ice, and he adds whatever fountain drink the guys wanted before setting them on a massive tray.

"Y'all are welcome to stay down there as long as you like and help yourself to any snacks."

"Thanks."

A loud grunt causes us both to turn around.

Ziggy walks toward us, adjusting his belt buckle. "Man, remind me never to order the special again."

Earl Ed shakes his head. "Most people who didn't grow up eating Enchilada can't stomach it."

Ziggy wipes his brow with the back of his hand, then slings his head so his shoulder-length hair flicks away from his eyes. "I believe that. How do they expect someone to function after such a meal?"

"Since the special includes a room at the inn, most people retreat to their room for the toilet," Earl Ed explains.

Ziggy leans against the counter and shakes his head. "Makes sense now."

"Ziggy, this is Earl Ed, by the way."

He extends a hand, and Earl Ed shakes it. "Ziggy, head cameraman."

"Earl Ed, this is my place."

Ziggy cocks his head toward the front room. "Nice pinball you got there."

"Thanks, you want a drink?"

"Just water. I think that margarita with the special was enough for now. Best clear out my system."

I bite back a laugh and refrain from commenting that I thought he just cleared out his system. Instead, I fill a cup with ice water and hand it to him.

"Thanks."

"We're downstairs, Ziggy." I point toward the stairs leading to the basement, then help Earl Ed stack the rest of the cups on the tray.

Ziggy goes ahead of us. Earl Ed's hand brushes mine when I hand him the last cup.

He half-smiles. "I was gonna tell you I have company coming over. I'll try not to disturb y'all."

"That's fine." I clear my throat and follow him downstairs.

After we deliver the drinks, Earl Ed retreats upstairs. I watch him leave and imagine his "company." Anyone coming by this late at night must be a date. Oddly enough, I find it unsettling.

Why should I care that an Alabama boy in overalls is entertaining another female upstairs? I shouldn't. So I force myself to get on with laying out the plans for tomorrow.

It's business as usual until we're halfway through discussing how we should set up the equipment in Carla's kitchen. Then I hear voices. Laughter, yelling, and more laughter. Maybe I'm under the nosy spell of Apple Cart, because I can't focus until I find out who's talking.

"Excuse me for a minute." I stand and go to the back door.

I've been warned someone was coming by and know this is none of my business. Still, I'm curious as to what type of woman Earl Ed dates. Does he prefer his women wear overalls, or have "more to love," as they say? He's always offering to feed me, so he may think I'm too skinny.

I open the door and stick my head out. The light outside is on, but I don't see anyone. I step out and turn my head. Something stings my butt like a bee.

"Ugh." I grab my backside and seethe with pain. Rubbing it does nothing but transfer orange paint to my hand. Apparently, I've been paintballed.

A guy wearing a welding mask and carrying a paintball gun comes out of nowhere. I want to run, but I hurt too bad to use my glutes.

I read "Heavy Metal, Apple Cart, Alabama" on his T-shirt when he comes closer. He pulls up his mask and starts apologizing. "I thought you was Earl Ed. I'm so sorry, miss." He puts his hand on my arm. "Are you all right? Need me to get you some ice?"

I shake my head. "I just need to hang tight a minute."

Earl Ed rushes down the hillside, almost falling a time or two. He's wearing goggles. "Mackenzie, what happened?"

More guys come from all directions, each wearing some sort of protective eye covering. Are they the company he told me about?

"I got hit in the . . . uh, hip area." I rub my butt cheek.

"Oh, I'm sorry." Earl Ed lifts his face from me toward the collective crowd. "Who did this?"

The welding guy speaks up. "I did, cuz. It was an accident. I thought she was you."

Earl Ed stares at him like he's lost his mind. "You're kidding, right?"

"Dude, I'm wearing a welding helmet."

"Well, that's your own stupid fault." Earl Ed shakes his head and puts his hands on my shoulders. "Mackenzie, are you okay?"

I nod. My butt is on fire, but the rest of me relaxes knowing he's here.

"What's going on?" Ziggy calls out behind me.

I step back to find the door open, with several of the crew members hanging their heads out.

I lift my painted hand. "I was hit by a paintball on accident."

"Paintball?" Rambo's excitement matches that of a kid approaching an ice cream truck rather than a middle-aged man approaching bedtime.

Earl Ed drops his hands from my shoulders. A chill covers my neck when it's no longer safe between his embrace.

"We paintball at least once a month." He narrows his eyes on the welding guy. "But someone had to get off course."

"Hey, you said not to mess up the lights. I didn't want to chance hitting them."

Earl Ed crosses his arms. "So you hit a random woman?"

Okay, I've only known the guy two days tops, but we are sharing living quarters for the next week. "Random" sounds a bit harsh.

The other guy shrugs. "I said I didn't mean to."

Earl Ed looks at me. "Sorry again. We'll head back to the course and let you guys be."

Rambo squeezes through the door past Ziggy. "Uh, Mackenzie, you ever heard of team building?"

"What about it?"

Rambo eyes the gun in the guy's hand. "Looks fun, don't you think?" His eyes trail to meet Earl Ed's. "Do you have more guns?"

Earl Ed laughs. "What do ya say, Mackenzie? Mind if these guys play us?"

I glance from Earl Ed to Rambo to Ziggy, then to the Heavy Metal guy. Every one of them has puppy eyes like they want this. I study Heavy Metal once more. Now *I* want this.

After a long day of prepping a new project and politely refusing "just one more cookie" from Carla while I showed the crew around her place, I could use a little stress relief. And I'd love to start with blasting the guy who lit up my butt like I've done five hundred squats.

"Only if I can play, too."

Earl Ed's cheeks raise into a wide grin. "Yes, ma'am."

Before I have time to process what I've agreed to, the entire crew is loading paintball guns as Earl Ed adjusts a pair of goggles on my head. He steps back and studies my face.

"Michael, trade with her."

He hands Earl Ed the welding helmet. Earl Ed removes my goggles and puts the massive mask over my head. "There, your pretty face won't get banged up now."

So he does think I'm pretty . . .

Not that it matters or that I even care. However, it's always nice to hear someone finds me attractive.

Earl Ed stands back and stares at me. I blink, trying to focus on him through the thick, scratchy surface over my eyes. He looks like a bearded blob, which doesn't give me much hope for zeroing in on targets.

"I would offer you some old clothes, but Michael here has already ruined your britches."

I thought he said something else until I remembered that britches is an actual synonym for pants, though one I don't hear in my everyday life.

"Thanks," I mutter behind the helmet.

Earl Ed goes over a list of simple rules with everyone. Rambo bounces on his heels like a puppy waiting on its owner to open the car door. After Earl Ed lays out the perimeters and stresses how the bubble lights are always off limits, he adds one more rule.

"Don't hit Mackenzie any closer than ten yards. We need to treat her like a lady."

I'm not sure whether I'm flattered, insulted, or scared. I decide I'm a little of all three and run for a tree when he yells "go."

CHAPTER FIVE

Earl Ed

I slather more butter on the skillet and pour pancake mix on top. My stomach growls as it sizzles in the pan. Then I remind myself that today is a low-carb day. I have to back down a notch on my eating after inhaling cookies on the way to the airport, then eating biscuits yesterday. At least bacon is keto-approved.

About the time the bacon finishes cooking, I hear footsteps down the hallway. Mackenzie enters with a yawn.

"Morning." I slap a dish towel over my shoulder and start transferring the bacon to a plate for the grease to drain.

"Good morning. What are you cooking for?"

"You."

She smiles. "That's so nice, but I could eat whatever craft services provides."

I shrug. "I have to eat, too, so I may as well cook for two." I clear my throat and hope that didn't come out in a weird way. Just in case she took it as flirty—or desperate—I add, "It's a lot easier to cook for more than one person."

That's true, which is why I often have a ton of leftovers. I snap my mouth shut before I say anything else awkward. Makenzie leans against the counter. "Need any help?"

I flip the last pancake. "Nope. You can go ahead and fix yourself a drink if you want. This is the last pancake."

She heads for the drink fountain, while I put all the pancakes on a large plate. I only made three so I wouldn't be tempted to eat any. I'm not sure how many women usually eat, but that seems like plenty for someone her size.

I toss some bacon on the side, then grab the rest of it for myself. When I cross into the dining area, she's fixing a second cup of ice.

"What do you want to drink?"

"Water's fine." I set our plates on a table and head to the kitchen for syrups.

After scanning the selection in my pantry, I grab all three varieties as well as some butter packets and a bottle of whipped cream. I'm not sure how she takes her pancakes.

I return to Mackenzie standing by the booth, staring at our plates. "Which one . . ."

"Oh, you have the pancakes."

She slides into the seat behind the pancake plate and arches an eyebrow. "You're only eating bacon?"

I waver my head and slide in my side. "I've been doing a low-carb thing some lately."

She nods.

I pull a few napkins from the dispenser at the edge of the table to relieve some nervous energy. "Anyway, I got some toppings for you. I can also cut up fruit if you want, or get some pecans or something."

She grins. "This is plenty, thank you."

I bite into a piece of bacon as she meticulously drips a

swirl of syrup onto her pancake stack. She adds a small dollop of whipped cream before cutting into it with her fork.

My phone buzzes in my shirt pocket. I pull it out and sigh when I read "Mama" on the screen. I answer. "Hello?"

"Earl Ed, I need your help."

I bite another piece of bacon and prepare to let her know I plan on staying at the business all day. "What is it?"

"I need you to catch a hog."

I drop the bacon on my plate and massage my temples. "Okay, soon as we finish eating."

"We who? Is Michael there? Because he could help, too."

"No, Mackenzie. I made her breakfast."

"Ohhh." Mama's voice is a mixture of dreamy and nosy.

I don't like it. She was way too excited when she thought Mackenzie was my girlfriend, then acted giddy again when I mentioned her staying in my spare room. Of course, she quickly offered her their full basement apartment. Then I told her the production rules against living on set.

That works in my favor, since staying with my mom might lead to more stories about me. I can picture her now, giving Mackenzie a tour of the basement while saying, "This is where Earl Ed slept when he still had an ankle monitor."

"So how long do you think you'll be?"

"Soon, bye." I hang up before she asks anything else.

Mackenzie licks syrup from her fork. I cut my eyes toward the window and away from two very strong temptations—Mackenzie's mouth and Golden Eagle Syrup.

When I do dare turn my eyes, I focus on her pancakes, which are mostly gone. I chew on my last bite of bacon and stare back at the window. "I'll drive you whenever you're ready. Mama wanted me to do something at her house."

"Okay, thanks. I'll text Ziggy and let him know I don't need a ride."

I suck down a large gulp of water and eat some of the ice.

One of the small luxuries that comes with living above an arcade is constant access to rat-turd ice, as we like to call it around here. The little square bits almost melt in your mouth.

Mackenzie takes one last bite of her pancake, and I study the drip of syrup on her lip. When she licks it from the corner of her mouth, I stand. With my lack of love life, this is torture.

"I'll go crank the truck." Not to rush her, but I can't afford to sit around and stare at her mouth.

I step outside, then back inside for a light jacket. One of the inconveniences about losing weight is that I lost my permanent body heat.

Mackenzie meets me at the stairs and climbs them beside me. I grab my coat while she grabs her purse, then we descend together.

I open her truck door first, then blow into my cold hands. "Sorry I didn't warm it up. I forgot my coat."

She shrugs and buckles her seat belt. "That's okay. This is nothing compared to New York."

She describes the harsh, nasty winters she's used to on the way to Mama's house. From New York to Canada, our weather is nothing to her. That makes me needing a coat even more emasculating.

We pull up to my parents' house, where Mama is swatting at the hog with a broom. It's ignoring her and eating her winter plants. I chuckle and park the truck.

"Make yourself at home. I've got to catch a pig."

Mackenzie cranes her neck for a better view of what's going on before getting out behind me. I lower the tailgate of my truck and pull a rope from the back.

"Mama, you may as well stop. That's not gonna do any good."

She drops the broom. "Oh, thank God, you're here. This

thing is ruining my flowers. I swear, if your G-Paw don't fix their fence soon."

"I can take it to Uncle Joey's dog pen on my way back."

"Thank you. I would've called your daddy, but he's at work."

I bite my tongue to refrain from saying I have my own business to run. Somehow she's confused me being "flexible" with "available."

The hog lifts its head and snorts. It's so fat, its eyes roll into a thin slither. With any luck, that heaviness translates into slowness. I make a slip knot on the end of the rope for a makeshift leash. Mama steps back as I go toward the hog. I wait for it to lower its head before making my move.

As the hog buries its snout in the bushes, I prepare the rope. Mackenzie cranes her neck from behind the hood of my truck. To someone unfamiliar with catching wild hogs, it might appear I intend on choking the poor thing to death.

Nope. We will wait and kill it on Christmas at the annual hog killing. For now I want to simply get it out of my mama's flowers.

I reach out and loop the rope around the hog's neck and tighten it enough for a lead rope. It turns back and snorts at me, then runs.

The rope ravels through my hand, burning my skin. I tighten my grip and hang on as the hog pulls me through the grass. In this case, fatness does not equate to slowness.

I dig my heels in the ground and finally get the animal to stop. Unfortunately, I had to straddle Mama's flag pole to do so. Well, I guess I can check fatherhood off my future plans.

"Ohhhh," I moan, closing my eyes, then grip the rope even tighter. Partly to not lose the pig and partly to release some tension from other areas.

The rope slacks up, and I open my eyes to a pair of black leather boots. I follow them up to Rambo's face. He's holding the rope. All one hundred pounds of Ziggy jogs over to help, too.

"Where do you want the pig?" Ziggy asks.

I cock my head toward my truck, where Mackenzie is plastered against the hood with her hands covering her mouth.

She and Mama rush toward me with faces full of concern once the guys push the hog toward the truck. By guys, I mean mainly Rambo.

Mackenzie reaches me first. "Oh my gosh. That was brutal." She kneels beside me and wraps an arm around my shoulder. Her hug is like a tiny weighted blanket that comforts me everywhere . . . except where I'm sure it will hurt for a while.

Mama bends by my other side. "Oh, son. Are you okay?" She tugs at my arm to help me up. Mackenzie helps, too, and together they pull me to standing.

I bend at the waist and moan again before answering my mother. "You may have to depend solely on Carly for grandkids."

"Oh, poor baby." She rubs my back, then takes my arm.

Mackenzie takes my other arm, and they walk me up the porch and inside. I glance over my shoulder on the way in the door to find that Rambo managed to get the hog in the truck bed.

They lead me to the couch, where I collapse, then wince at the pain of landing too hard, too fast.

"I'll get you some ice." Mama frowns at me sympathetically, then looks out the window. "And I'll call Robin to see if Liam can drive the hog to his house."

"No!" I shoot up, causing myself more pain, then lie back slowly. "I'd rather drive my truck like this than have him drive it."

She frowns again. "Well, I'll call your daddy, then."

Finally. It takes a pig near castrating me for her to disturb Daddy.

I lean up to grab a pillow from the chair beside me and meet a camera lens like a deer in the headlights. One of the crew members is filming me.

"How long have you been filming?"

"Uh . . ." He leans back and checks the camera. "Long enough to get some sweet B-roll."

Mackenzie turns off the camera and ushers him out the front door. I lean against the pillow and close my eyes. Looks like I might need Liam after all to help with Double Drive.

Mackenzie

I had a hard time leaving Earl Ed on Carla's couch. Before we left to shoot an event, he insisted all he needed was rest and a new pack of ice for his groin. Still, I can't help but sympathize.

The only other time I've witnessed someone hit a flag pole that hard with their privates was when my friend talked me into trying pole-dancing aerobics.

Carla turns on her blinker at a marquee sign with "Wisteria High School" in faded blue print. Ziggy switches our turn signal, and we follow her into a large parking lot.

Something rumbles behind me. I turn to Rambo holding his stomach.

I narrow my eyes. "What did you guys eat for breakfast?"

"Mainly coffee, and the cookies Carla gave us before leaving. Nobody wanted to try the breakfast burritos at Enchilada."

"What happened to craft services?"

Ziggy shakes his head. "Production gave us per diem instead. Said it was hard enough to get all of us to come out this far, and those people don't make near what the rest of us do."

I shrug and make a mental note to tell them about the food at Double Drive. During open hours, of course. I'd hate to impose on Earl Ed even more. Plus, I secretly have enjoyed our quiet meals together.

We hit a large pothole, bouncing everyone a few inches off their seats. Rambo juggles his coffee tumbler, while some of the other crew scramble to secure equipment.

"My bad," Ziggy calls to everyone behind him.

I look up from my notebook at the parking lot. That pothole wasn't an isolated incident. This ground could double as a war zone—post attack.

Ziggy does a great job weaving around the larger holes until a cop car pulls up behind us and flashes its lights. We're already close to Carla's parked SUV, so I signal to Ziggy that we may as well stop.

He curses and rolls down the window. I close the cover of my notes and prepare to explain where we're from. In a place this small, the out-of-state tag on our rental van likely raised suspicion.

A tall man in uniform struts up and tips his tan cowboy hat. He's good looking, but in the annoying way that says he knows it. "Morning. I'm afraid I have to ask the driver to exit the vehicle."

I open the glove box and dig for paperwork on the rental while Ziggy gets out. By the time I locate the registration info as well as the rental receipt, Ziggy is arguing with the cop as he walks across a faded parking space line.

"What's going on?" I ask.

"Well, howdy, ma'am." The cowboy cop tips his hat again, then extends his hand. "Sheriff Bradley Manning."

I glance at his hand before giving it a quick, firm shake. Then I fan the paperwork toward him. "This is the registration information, and a receipt for renting the vehicle."

He drops his eyes toward the paper, then takes his time raising them to my eyes. "Ma'am, I'm more concerned about your husband's driving."

"He's not my husband."

"Boyfriend?"

"We're not together." I waver my head. "I mean we're here together."

Ziggy interrupts. "I'm head of her film crew."

"So y'all aren't together?" He raises the brim of his hat and studies my face.

I cross my arms. "What is this about?"

"Oh." The sheriff cocks his head toward Ziggy. "His drunken driving."

"I haven't had anything today except for coffee and water."

Bradley gets within inches of Ziggy's face and sniffs. "What did you put in that coffee?"

I uncross my arms and come between them. "This is absurd. He was trying to dodge the dozens of potholes in this parking lot." I point to the van. "We have expensive equipment in there."

"Tell you what, miss. Since I like you, I'm gonna let this one slide if he passes a Breathalyzer test."

"Fine." I grit my teeth, trying to forget where his eyes landed when he said he liked me.

Bradley pulls a Breathalyzer from his car and hands it to Ziggy. The results prove he has no alcohol in his system. Bradley puts the tester back in his car and adjusts his hat.

"I apologize. You're free to go." He points to Ziggy, then me. "Unless you folks need a police escort for your filming."

"I think we're good," I say.

"Great, see y'all around." He climbs in his car and heads the opposite direction.

I roll my eyes and go to the van. The rest of the crew shuffles to sit back down when I approach the door, as if they weren't plastered to the back window taking everything in a minute earlier.

"Okay, crew, let's roll."

My rag tag team of men with equipment files out one by one like the suitors leaving a limo on a reality dating show. Except instead of suits, they're wearing jeans, baggy athletic pants, or cargo shorts. But that's only the beginning of what sets them apart from a charming bachelor.

We cross a few more potholes, this time on foot, before we reach Carla. She's unloading cookies from the back of her vehicle with the help of an attractive young woman.

The woman smiles at me and pushes her brown bangs to the side. "You must be Mackenzie."

"I am." I smile, then study her leather vest filled with combs. I sincerely hope—

"I'm Adrianne, the cosmetologist helping with Carla's hair and makeup."

"Great!" I was told by the producer Carla recommended someone local. Honestly, I'm relieved to find someone so fashionable in such a small town.

Carla grins. "Adrianne does my hair all the time, so I encouraged her to apply."

I sigh. This is a small victory, but one I could use after the cop incident. "I'm so glad. Adrianne, I want Carla to look her natural, pretty self, with maybe a little heavier makeup on when indoors for lighting and filming purposes."

She nods. "Just like a beauty pageant."

"Sure." Having never participated in a pageant, I'll have to trust her judgment.

The women continue gathering trays, and I call Dougy over to take some of the larger ones. He's the lowest man on the totem pole, since he's barely nineteen and this is his first film job.

Between Quality Inn, the impromptu paintball fight, and getting pulled over by a cop for dodging potholes, it wouldn't surprise me if he changed his major to something more predictable once his second semester starts.

"Thank you." Carla smiles at us and leads us down a slight hill toward the entrance to a football stadium.

I hear a cow mooing nearby, but don't give it much thought after watching goats and a hog graze freely in Carla's yard. I've come to expect random farm animals wandering around Wisteria.

Another attractive guy rushes toward Carla with a clipboard. That's more attractive men than I expected to see in one day per the population of this town.

He wipes a hand over his dark hair and sighs. "Hey, Mrs. Carla. You're right on time. We're not going to serve refreshments until the eagle has landed."

"Great. Here's the film crew I told you about."

He shakes my hand, then Ziggy's. "Nice to meet y'all. I'm Kyle Tolbert."

His eyes lock on Adrianne's, and he blushes. "Adrianne."

She gives him a tight-lipped smile. "Kyle."

Kyle clears his throat and stares down at his clipboard. He puffs out his cheeks before facing us again. "If y'all will follow me, I can get you access to the field."

"Thanks." We follow Kyle past bleachers filled with spectators.

As I'm craning my neck to study the crowd, I hear another moo. I turn to the field, where a large cow is meandering around the end zone. A few people stand by the fence, but nobody is on the field.

Kyle leads us to a table, where we place the cookies. Then he opens the gate to the field and motions for us to follow. I stretch an eyebrow at Ziggy, who shrugs. We enter the field, and Kyle shuts the gate.

"I thought y'all might want to set up on the sidelines. That should give a good bird's eye view of the poop."

I swallow. "Pardon me?"

Kyle steps to his right and swings his arm as if I wanted to pass. "Go ahead."

I shake my head. "No, I mean, did you say poop?"

Carla fans a cow cookie my way, and for the first time, I notice a chocolate morsel by its tail. My mouth opens as I realize my mistake.

"Whoa, I assumed cow patty meant hamburgers."

Kyle grins and shakes his head. "No, ma'am." He taps the clipboard in his hand. "We make a chart to represent those numbers on the field. People pay for squares, and the winner is whoever picked the number where the cow poops."

I glance across the field and notice it's painted similar to a checkerboard, with numbers inside. Then I turn to Kyle. "But why?"

"To raise money for the Angel Tree."

"Angel Tree?" I could really use a dictionary of Southern events and occasions.

"It's a charity where we collect money and gifts for families in need," Carla explains.

"Oh, well that's nice." That part I get. The whole betting on a cow to poop, I don't.

This is why Alabama needs a lottery. When people can't go to the Quick Stop and buy scratchers, they'll put money on whatever they can, like where they think a cow might poop.

"And you make cookies for this every year, Carla?"

"This is actually my first year. Until last Christmas, we only did the cow-patty drop pre-football season."

Kyle smiles at the cookie in Carla's hand, then nods toward the spectators. "We didn't expect so many people to stay and watch last year. Turns out some were afraid we'd move the poop to fudge the results."

I choke down a hint of vomit at the idea of someone purposely moving animal poop for any reason other than walking a dog in a public park.

"It only seemed natural to have Mrs. Carla's cookies here as a nice little treat while people wait."

I force a smile to unfurl my nose. "Sounds great," I lie. "Ziggy, why don't you set up in front of the fifty-yard line and go ahead and interview Carla and Kyle about the event."

Ziggy gives me a thumbs-up before instructing his crew.

Dougy pauses by Kyle as he's carrying an armful of extension cords. "Hey, you got any open squares I can bet on?"

Kyle pulls a pen from the edge of the clipboard and shuffles through some papers. "A few."

Dougy loops the cords around his arm to free a hand for signing his name and digging money from his wallet. I hope it works out for him, since I'm not convinced anything else in this job will.

Carla is a pro at working the crowd. Ziggy follows her through the bleachers as she passes out cookies and catches up with neighbors. We have another camera set up to get the cow.

Not since I dealt with a monkey in a real estate commercial have I worked with an unpredictable animal. The dogs on Hallmark are top-notch and have spoiled me.

I peer around the cookie table at another crowd gathered near a circular fence. "What's over there?"

"That's the skating rink," Kyle answers.

"Huh." I fight the urge to roll my eyes at a small-town Christmas function having an ice-skating rink.

One plus for the cow-poop contest is its originality.

"Dougy, come with me to shoot some B-roll."

Dougy's face lights up like Carla's front lawn. "Really?"

"Yeah." His excitement warms me. So many people in this industry are jaded. Yet another sign he won't make it.

He picks up a camera and follows me. As we come closer to the other fence, collective humming noises ring out. Not in the sense of a gang of hummingbirds. Gang? That can't be right. Group, pack? Whatever. Regardless, this humming is deeper and louder and way more annoying.

When we reach the fence, I see that it's not an actual fence. Rather, it's a circle of box fans curved around frozen ground.

A young girl with pink hair flags me down as I walk past the table. "You need a ticket to go in there."

"I'm with a film crew. We're not here to skate."

She picks at her black fingernails and pokes out her bottom lip. "Doesn't matter. Rules say you gotta buy a ticket to pass."

I pull out a card, and she snickers. "Cash only."

"You're kidding."

"Nope." She points a long, dark nail to a sign duct-taped on the side of her table. In thin ink, it reads, "Cash only."

I sigh and dig in my pockets. Sometimes I keep cash in my coat pocket for coffee or food truck runs when I'm too busy to swipe a card. Nope. Nothing.

"Dougy, do you have any cash on you?"

He shakes his head. "I did, until I bought three chances on that heifer."

"Uh, miss?" I turn to the girl.

She folds her arms. "You're welcome to tape from out here on the other side of this table."

I nod, then pull Dougy back a foot. "Just zoom in, this is B-roll anyway." I twist my mouth at the massive fans. "And it's not like we can hear what anyone is saying."

This shot is destined to become a montage of ice skating set to Christmas music. So much for avoiding cliché small-town Christmas.

CHAPTER SIX

Earl Ed

Well, what do you know? Bradley's Santa suit zips with ease, and I even need a little stuffing. This all-bacon diet has paid off. Maybe I should write a diet book. Nah, it would be too short.

Eat bacon. The end.

I adjust the fake beard over my own. Bradley stressed how Santa needed a long, white beard rather than a short, brown one for authenticity. It itches, but not near as badly as the hat.

Something tells me Bradley added this task to my community service requirement out of spite.

As soon as I exit the civic center, he walks up, grinning ear to ear. Yeah, he totally did this out of spite.

"Did this beard itch when you wore it?" I lean beside my truck and scratch under the fake beard.

He shrugs. "I haven't played Santa in two Christmases."

He steps in front of me and straightens the beard. "Guy who wore it last year had a run in with a cat. Maybe there's some fur left up in there."

Bradley gets within an inch of my face and digs through the beard like he's doing a lice check. I stiffen and close my eyes.

After the most awkward moment since sharing a jail cell with a mafia hitman, Bradley steps back. "False alarm. Must be dust from where I stored it."

I start to ask where he stored it, then decide I don't want to know. Instead, I tug the collar of my coat a little higher to create a buffer between my skin and the beard.

Bradley pats me on the back. "You'll do great."

I slide away from his hand and fiddle with some of the gifts in the back of my truck. He doesn't take the hint, and instead follows me.

"If you need any tips on—" He stops mid-sentence and cranes his neck to see around me. "Gotta go."

What a relief. I turn to find Ashley from the bank carrying a large box toward the civic center. Bradley catches up and takes the box in for her. Pretty women are his kryptonite.

Speaking of pretty women, Mackenzie crosses the parking lot. Heat rises up my neck as her eyes scan my Santa suit. Not my best look.

"Look at you!" She smiles.

I force a grin, though I doubt she can see it through two layers of facial hair. "Thanks."

"Carla told me you're playing Santa for a children's home."

"Something like that." I'm delivering gifts to a large foster home while dressed like Santa, so I guess that counts.

"Is it okay if we tag along and take them some cookies, maybe video their reactions?"

I shrug. "Fine by me."

I close the tailgate on my truck and resist the urge to snatch off the beard. If I take it off now, there's no way I'll put it back on before seeing the kids.

"Great. I'll get Ziggy to follow us with your mom and some cookies."

"Follow *us*?"

Her smile fades a bit. "That is, if you don't mind me riding with you."

"No, that's fine." I suck in a breath. My words came out a little too anxious. "I'll wait here." This time I lower my voice to hide any emotion.

She blinks, possibly at my voice flip-flopping like a pubescent kid. Then she turns and heads inside.

After a few minutes of trying to ignore the itch on my neck, she returns with Ziggy and my mom, who's holding a large platter. Mama and Ziggy get in her car with the camera and cookies, while Mackenzie climbs in beside me.

We ride in silence on the way to the children's home, except for when Mackenzie points out background shots she wants to get later. The blow-up Santa dancing in the wind on top of Piggly Wiggly makes the cut.

I study her from the corner of my eye. One skill I picked up in the slammer was facing one eye forward while slanting the other toward my cellmate. It came in handy when I needed to protect my few belongings. Never would I have guessed I could later use it to check out girls.

Once we hit the dirt road, Mackenzie puts away her pen and paper. She grabs on to the handle above her door. The presents bounce in the bed as I navigate across a few potholes too large to miss.

A large cedar tree greets us at the end of the driveway. Its lights are already on, reflecting the sunshine.

I park near the farmhouse and get out. Mackenzie

follows, her jaw dropping as her eyes trail the house.

"This place is beautiful. I've seen several like it shooting Hallmark movies, but never so homey."

"It's the real deal." I open the tailgate and start unloading gifts.

Mama and Ziggy pull up. He helps me empty the truck bed before unloading the camera. I line up the riding toys beside the truck and sling the big bag of wrapped gifts over my shoulder.

I grunt as the sack hits my back. This Santa gig is starting to feel more like a CrossFit workout.

Mama gathers her platter of cookies, then stands still for Mackenzie to smooth down her hair.

"I'm no Adrianne, but you look great."

Mama beams and pats Mackenzie on the cheek.

Mackenzie returns her smile, then turns to me. "We're ready."

Okay . . .

"Go on in." Mackenzie nods.

Ziggy picks up the camera, alerting me that she wants to film us walking. As if dressed head to toe like Santa weren't awkward enough. Okay, more like head to ankle, since I'm wearing my own brown work boots. If any of the kids question them, I'll say they haven't been in soot yet.

We climb the porch, and I stumble slightly on the top step. It's a little wobbly, and this bag of gifts hasn't gotten any lighter.

Mackenzie prompts me to knock on the door. I do and try not to focus on my itchy beard as I wait on someone to answer.

A man a little older than me opens the door. He welcomes us in until he spots Ziggy's camera. With one hand, he shoves Ziggy back on the porch, and with the other, he slams the door.

"What are y'all doing with that camera?"

Ziggy lowers the camera and twists the toothpick in his mouth to the other side. "Uh, filming?"

The guy narrows his eyes, and Mackenzie steps between him and Ziggy.

She extends a hand. "Hi, I'm Mackenzie Magee, and I'm directing a show about Carla Mayberry's Christmas cookies. We brought a batch for your family."

He crosses his arms and stands more squarely in front of the door. "We can't even photograph these kids' faces. They're in foster care."

She nods. "I understand and respect that. Could we possibly shoot Earl Ed and Carla walking in the door and then interview you . . ." Mackenzie shakes her palms toward him. "Or your wife, if you prefer, about the children's home?"

He twists his mouth and stares at his boots before looking at her. "I suppose."

Mackenzie clasps her hands in front of her. "Thank you so much, Mr. . . ."

"Just call me Andy."

"Thanks, Andy." Mackenzie extends her hand once more, and this time he shakes it.

He opens the door and steps aside for us to enter.

A group of wide-eyed kids greets me soon as I cross the threshold. A skinny woman in a festive sweater walks up and smiles.

"Hi, I'm Lina, and you must be Santa." She winks, then stands beside her husband.

"Ho, ho, ho, pleased to meet you, ma'am." I face the kids and drop the bag from my sore shoulder. "And pleased to meet all y'all!"

A tiny girl with pigtails comes up and wraps around my leg. I reach down and pat her back. "Want to be Santa's elf?"

She lifts her head and grins. I kneel to shake her from my leg, and because I refuse to lift that bag again until it's empty.

She gasps when I open the sack and pull out the first gift. I'm relieved to find them all labeled, since I know none of these kids.

"Timmy," I read off the first tag. The little girl takes the gift from me and bounces across the room to a boy a little bigger than her.

He takes the gift, and all eyes turn to him as he opens it. He smiles when there's enough wrapping gone to see it's a huge Lego set.

I continue handing out gifts until every kid has one. A few times, I catch a glimpse of Mackenzie smiling. As I bend for the empty bag, I lock eyes with her. We share a look until something tugs at my beard.

Before I can stand, the itchy contraption falls from my face. I break eye contact with Mackenzie to find a cat rolling around with my beard like a ball of yarn.

Some kids gasp and others laugh. I sling my arm over my face, but not soon enough. One boy points to me and screams, "I told y'all the real Santa does too have a brown beard, just like last year."

I'm not sure what that means, but Mama starts passing out cookies like they're candy. Which they kind of are.

Maddy, the small girl who helped me, stares at my face, tears welling in her eyes. I cup my hands around my own beard and back toward the door. All the other kids are focused on their gifts and couldn't care less if I even have a beard. But I can't kill the magic for Maddy just yet. She's too innocent and starry eyed.

I'm almost out the door when my boot catches on the threshold. I stumble backward a few steps, then fall on my butt and tumble down the front porch.

The air leaves my chest when I hit the ground with a

heavy thump. I struggle to catch my breath, then lift to my elbows. Before I can stand, Mackenzie is at my side, helping me to my feet.

"Thanks." I dust grass from the Santa suit.

"Welcome." She nods toward my truck. "I think we should leave the interviews to Ziggy."

"Agreed." I stagger toward my truck like an off-duty bull rider.

So much for fulfilling community service by playing Santa.

Mackenzie

"And I make sure the rear end of every reindeer has a perky little tail." Carla dollops white frosting into a perfect swoop resembling the backside of a white-tail deer, then smiles at the camera.

I can see why the network wanted to make a Christmas special with her. If Pioneer Woman and Santa Claus had a love child, it would be her.

Ziggy zooms in on the cookie as she places it on a platter with the others. Carla reaches for an unfrosted snowman-shaped cookie, when heavy footsteps cause us all to turn.

Earl Ed stops at the kitchen entrance with one of those earmuff hats like Cousin Eddie wears in the *Christmas Vacation* movie. The ear flaps are halfway between up and down, standing at a ninety-degree angle.

"What?" He narrows his eyes, and I blink.

My staring at his weird hat could easily be mistaken for

staring at *him*. As always, I revert to sarcasm when nervous or embarrassed.

"No Santa suit today?"

He chuckles. "That was a one-time occurrence, I'm afraid." His face lifts into a grin. "Unless you'd like for me to wear it again."

Well, that sarcastic comment backfired. My face flames, and I turn toward Carla and the array of cookies spread across the countertops.

Ziggy clears his throat. "If you two don't mind, we have one more cookie to frost, then we can pack up for the parade."

I half-smile at Ziggy. "Go ahead."

He instructs Carla to continue with the snowman decorating, while I lean against a different counter and watch. I catch a glimpse of Earl Ed from the corner of my eye. That stupid hat makes him look like a park ranger on a retro cartoon. But it also gives him this rugged mountain man appearance in the weirdest way.

Ugh, what is going on here? I focus my attention on the sugar cookie snowman. Too bad my mind drifts where my eyes can't. *Was he flirting with me a minute ago? Even more importantly, was I flirting with him?*

What has gotten into me? Nothing makes sense about me flirting with a guy in rural Alabama while I'm directing a show where his mom is the star.

"And cut." Ziggy steals my line, but in his defense, I was somewhere besides reality.

I help Carla gather what she plans on taking to Mary's Diner, where she said everyone eats snacks after the parade.

A natural camera personality, Carla breaks character for the first time since we started filming. She greets Earl Ed when he crosses the kitchen. "Hi, son. Thanks for coming."

"No problem."

I stare at the cookies in front of me while listening to their conversation.

"We need these taken out carefully, and placed in the side room at Mary's. I'll arrange them once we're there."

Carla slides a massive Tupperware container toward her son, then meticulously lines another container with parchment paper to add more cookies.

I stack the box of cookies more precisely after realizing how meticulous she's being. After gathering countless cookies and Ziggy loading the van, Earl Ed slides the last of the containers into the back of his truck.

"You really outdid yourself this year, Mama."

"I had to make plenty since I'm the grand marshal this year."

I smirk at the memory of Bradley offering her the title when he found out we were filming the parade. Once I began talking transportation options, he corrected himself by saying she would actually ride with him and share the honors.

We follow Earl Ed into town, and Ziggy parks the van behind his truck at the General Store. Adrianne waves at me when I get out. I join her and give my opinion on her lipstick options for Carla.

"This is my favorite. Good choice." Adrianne smiles. She rolls the burgundy tube up and starts smearing Carla's lips.

I survey all the various floats and cars in the parking lot. My eyes widen when they land on a wooden sign above the storefront that reads, "From a cradle to a coffin." That's disturbing.

Perhaps even more disturbing than Bradley driving up on a tractor decorated with a wreath and Christmas lights. He's wearing a Santa hat on top of his cowboy hat, along with a Christmas scarf.

He hops down. "Looking good, Mrs. Mayberry." He

nods to Adrianne. "Maybe you could work on me sometime?"

Adrianne reaches into her case of makeup and pulls out a huge powder puff. She bops Bradley square on the nose. He coughs and sneezes, then wipes the creamy powder off on his shirtsleeve. I make eye contact with Earl Ed, who is either terribly constipated or desperately trying not to laugh.

Bradley clears his throat as if to erase the encounter and holds a hand out to Carla. "Mrs. Mayberry, would you care to join me as my co-marshal?"

Carla giggles and takes his hand. I suspect he charms a lot of older women in town. He helps her onto the tractor, where she sits on a tiny seat beside the driver's seat.

"Want me to go ahead and take the cookies to Mary's?" Earl Ed asks.

"That would be great," Carla answers.

"Ziggy, why don't you film Carla during the parade and have some of the guys get B-roll of the whole thing. I'll go with Earl Ed and set up the cookie display."

Carla smiles. "Great idea. That will save me some time."

I grin at her. "No problem."

"Let's go." Earl Ed opens the passenger door to his truck.

I climb inside and admire more floats pulling into the parking lot. "Is it always this festive?"

"Yeah." He laughs. "I'm sure you're plenty used to festive living in New York."

I shrug. "It's different, but you guys are just as festive, if not more in a way."

"What do you mean?"

I glance out the window at the huge blow-up Santa tied to the roof of Piggly Wiggly. "Everyone here seems to get in the Christmas spirit. There it's more commercialized and methodical."

"I guess I never thought of it like that. Mama and Aunt

Robin have always wanted to go to New York at Christmas."

"What about you?" My tongue tingles when the words leave my mouth. I'm not sure why I asked him about going to New York.

Earl Ed smirks. "Too many people. I about had a panic attack in the Atlanta airport."

"Really?"

He pulls in front of the restaurant and parks the truck. "Yeah." He removes his hat and tosses it on the dash. The furry sides stare back at us like the backside of roadkill. Which, by the way, I have seen my fair share of in real life since coming here.

"Ever since I got out of jail, being in huge crowds overwhelms me."

I crane my head toward the nearby church, where a large group of people is gathering with camping chairs. "What about tonight?"

"Nah. I know everyone around here. In jail, I either had to watch my back or was in isolation. So strangers make me hypersensitive."

My heart aches for what he must've gone through, especially considering his only crime was mishandling mail. "What about me and the crew?"

"No, not at all. Y'all are great. Besides, I wouldn't call you a stranger now."

I smile. "Not with me sleeping down the hall."

"No." He smiles, too, and his eyes glimmer the slightest bit.

My heart speeds up as we lock eyes, then something loud rustles in the truck bed. We both turn our heads to an older guy who I vaguely recognize.

"Paul!" Earl Ed jumps out and rushes to the back of the truck. I follow.

"What are you doing?" Earl Ed asks.

Paul drops the Tupperware container and runs in the opposite direction.

Earl Ed swipes his hand across his face and picks up the container. "That guy will do anything for free food."

"Isn't he the one from mini golf?"

"That's the one." Earl Ed shakes his head. "If you don't mind getting the door, we'll take these inside."

I help him transport the cookies. An older lady greets us and introduces herself as Mary. She leads me to a table with a red-checkered tablecloth where I can showcase the cookies.

Unfortunately, several are broken inside the bin Paul dropped. I hold up a legless Santa and sigh. "Your poor mother."

Earl Ed takes the container of misfit toys in edible form. "You put out the pretty ones. I got this."

I raise a brow, questioning where he's going with this. But he waves me away and takes the cookies to a nearby table.

We work in silence for the next few minutes. When I finish the display, I stand back and admire the non-broken cookies. Just in time, too, as the door opens and a crowd rushes toward our area of the restaurant.

Slight panic kicks in as I search the crowd for Carla and Ziggy. They fight their way toward us, and Ziggy starts the camera. People form a line beside the table of sweets, then stop when Earl Ed lets out a whistle. Somewhere, a stray dog's ears are bleeding right now.

Everyone stares, and he points to the plate of broken cookies. Carla gasps, and Ziggy zooms in on the plate.

"We thought it would be fun to make a cookie puzzle for the kids. Grab a cookie and see which of your friends has the missing piece."

A few kids rush over to the broken cookies, and Carla sighs. I shoot Earl Ed a smile laced with a sincere thank you.

CHAPTER SEVEN

Mackenzie

I wrap my scarf a different way, then pull it off entirely. It's silly to wear wool around my neck in sixty-five-degree weather, even if it makes a festive fashion statement.

This is the first time I've put any thought into what I wear for a shoot. However, it's also the first time I've directed a scene at the star actor's mother-in-law's house with the entire family present.

Okay, so scenarios like that happen all the time in scripted movies. But it's never the actress's real mother-in-law, because she is a real actress. Reality TV is a whole new game for me.

I toss the scarf on my bed and glance out the window. Earl Ed is still outside messing with go-karts. His business closed for Christmas as of last night. Without giving it another thought, I hurry downstairs to the go-kart track.

He straightens when he notices my feet beside him. "Hey, Mackenzie."

"Hey, this Christmas thing tonight at your G-Maw's, what should I wear?"

He wipes sweat from his brow and laughs. "No dress code, trust me."

"Yeah, but like will most people be casual or kind of dressy, or festive?"

He drops a wrench and sighs. "Let's see. My Aunt Misty will have on something way too tight and not age appropriate. Her husband will wear some stupid Christmas sweater like the stepdad from *The Santa Clause*. Her daughter will have on so little you can barely call it clothes. Daddy will probably have a gun holster on his belt, and Liam will be head-to-toe in camo."

My eyes widen with every description as I try and imagine the scene in my head. "So I can wear whatever."

"Yep, pretty much. And don't worry about a gift. I got you covered." He winks.

"Gift?" My stomach pings. "I'm supposed to bring a gift for G-Maw?" I've heard rumors of Southerners going overboard on hospitality etiquette, but I wasn't prepared to take part in it.

"Nah, not like that. We play Dirty Santa."

"Dirty Santa?" I hope this has something to do with mud and not the other kind of dirty.

"Not like you're thinking."

I blink, and my body tenses with embarrassment. What did he think I was thinking? Maybe the mud thing. Please be the mud thing. I hold my breath and prepare an explanation. Luckily, he keeps talking, which helps kill the awkwardness swarming inside me.

"We each bring a cheap gift and draw numbers to take

turns opening them. When it's your turn, you can open a gift or steal someone else's."

"Oh, like White Elephant."

He nods. "Dirty Santa, White Elephant. Y'all, you all. Tomato, tomato. It's all the same. Just different names."

"Nobody I know says tomoto."

"Well, whatever *you all* call things."

He sounds genuinely mad, and I laugh. After a cold stare for a few seconds, he laughs, too.

Once the laughter dies down, he bends and picks up the wrench, then starts doing something to the go-kart.

I turn to leave, but stop. Maybe it's from sheer boredom or curiosity, but I stare at the overturned go-kart.

"If you're just gonna stand there, hand me those screws."

My shoulder flinches. I didn't mean to come off as creepy, or lazy, or just plain weird. Although I'm the latter of those a lot. I scramble to grab the pile of screws behind him.

His large, calloused fingers graze my palm as he scoops them from my hand. "Thanks."

I ball up my empty hand as if I can keep the warmth and comfort of his touch on my palm forever. After a few seconds of staring at my fist, I glance back at him.

"What's wrong with it?" My cheeks redden as I try to feign interest in the go-kart work. Better that than admit I want to stay busy to keep my mind off meeting his family.

Not that it should matter what they think of me. I'm the woman director here to capture Carla's cookie story, then run back to New York. I know that's what they think of me, because I overheard Carla's husband use those exact words to describe me to someone over the phone.

I'm not sure if it's Carla, Earl Ed, or the fact that I'm dealing with real people instead of actors. Regardless, I want G-Maw and the other family members to like me. Besides, if they don't, it can make filming extra stressful.

"I'm cleaning the carburetor."

"Oh." I start to ask what that is, but spout out something equally stupid instead. "Do you need a driver's license to drive these?"

He smiles at me and chuckles. "You've never driven a go-kart?"

I shrug. "Well, no. I've never driven anything."

His jaw drops. "For real?"

I nod. "Yeah. Remember, I don't have a license."

He stands and cocks his head toward me like I'm some rare animal behind bars at the zoo. "Yeah, but like not even a bike?"

I roll my eyes. "I've ridden a bicycle."

"Well, you did say anything."

I sigh. "I meant with a motor."

He tosses the wrench in a nearby toolbox. "Want to drive one?"

The row of working go-karts glistens in the afternoon sun. This isn't something I'd normally do, but after my spontaneous paintball battle, I'm beginning to understand why some people gravitate toward outdoor entertainment. I tend to grab a book or go to dinner instead, but I can't deny my interest in speeding around the concrete curves.

"Sure."

Earl Ed claps his hands together loudly as if starting a slow clap. He swings an arm around my shoulder and leads me toward the row of cars.

My stomach knots at the idea of driving, but his arm curled around me brings a bit of comfort. I relax under his arm, knowing whatever happens to the go-kart—or me—he can fix it. I hope . . .

As a tinge of doubt starts to bubble in the back of my mind, he pulls a shiny black go-kart from the line of two-seaters.

I grin. "This is the best-looking one."

"I thought you might say that."

"How come?"

He scans me head to toe. "You're wearing black again. It's either black or brown with you, and I don't have a brown one."

I fold my arms across my black sweater, which hangs over black leggings. He's right, all the way to my black boots. I'm torn between taking offense that he made fun of my colorless clothes or flattered that he noticed what I wear.

Earl Ed pulls a rope and the go-kart hums. I jump back a few inches, not expecting the loud roar. The sound levels out, and he motions for me to sit in the driver's seat. He gets into the passenger side.

"This is the brake, and this is the gas." He points out a few more tips about the steering and how it helps to ease off the pedals rather than lower and lift my foot abruptly.

My neck itches as nervous energy trickles up my spine. I shove my sweater sleeves up to my elbows before gripping the wheel and sigh with relief that I took off that stupid scarf. It would've added some color to my monochromatic wardrobe, but it was hot.

"Okay, any questions?"

Instead of answering him with words, I step on the gas pedal and bolt down the hill. The side of the track is lined with tires, and I realize why when I run head-on into one and bounce off the side.

"Whoa."

"That's okay. You weren't going too fast. You just need to learn how to steer."

"How do I back up?"

Without saying anything, he hops out and jerks the back of the go-kart, spinning it to face the road.

I'm both scared and a little turned on at how effortlessly

he can move a metal machine with me inside. He hops back in the passenger seat as if it were nothing.

"You can't get hurt in this thing." He wavers his head. "Unless, of course, you flip us multiple times and we bounce over the railing, off the retaining wall, and onto the asphalt behind the basement."

I swallow. "Thanks for that visual."

He laughs. "But that's the worst that could happen."

"I should hope so."

"You'll be fine. Just keep both hands on the wheel."

Earl Ed takes my hands in his and gently places them on either side of the steering wheel. His big hands cover mine completely and are somehow soft despite the calluses. Before he moves them, I turn toward him.

He leans down not even an inch. Just enough to make me question if he might want to kiss me, or if I'd want him to want to kiss me. I decide to lean an inch closer and test my theory.

When I do, my foot shoves onto the gas, and we barrel down the hill. *Steer!* My heart races from the anticipation of a kiss turning into the anticipation of a wreck. It kicks my reflexes into overdrive, and I jerk the wheel as the road curves. Then I overcorrect by jerking the wheel the opposite direction.

We hit another wall of tires, and the go-kart bounces back. My head spins, and the seat belt cinches against my hips. I breathe like a marathon runner on the last leg of the race.

Earl Ed puts a hand on my shoulder and stares at me, concern all over his face. "Are you all right?"

I nod, still too breathless to answer. After a minute of him staring at me, I manage to say, "I think I'm done with driving."

He bursts out laughing and drops his hand from my

shoulder. The tension between us breaks, and I laugh along with him.

What was I thinking?

I have no business trying to drive—or kiss my Uber driver/temporary landlord/show star's son.

Earl Ed

"I'll ride with you."

I lift my head from pouring a thermos full of tea to look at Mackenzie, wearing a bright red sweater with a red-and-green scarf. Hmm . . . maybe my comment about black and brown didn't put her off.

"You look nice."

"Thanks." Either the red has reflected onto her face, or she's blushing.

"Welcome." I screw the lid on my thermos and circle the counter.

After the holidays, I need to focus on finishing my apartment kitchen. Coming downstairs for sweet tea is getting old.

"I'm ready if you are." I sip my tea and savor every bit of sweetness.

Even though sweet tea is my usual splurge, I still can't drink G-Maw's. One glass contains more sugar than I've had in the last month.

Mackenzie smiles and follows me outside. It's a little cooler than before, but not cool enough for a jacket. Especially when going to G-Maw's. The entire family, plus more, will pack in that place like a can of sardines, kicking the body heat into overdrive.

I automatically reach to open Mackenzie's door for her, but she beats me to it. I half-grin at her before circling the truck to my side. Even though I'm technically her Uber for the evening, it seems rude not to open the door for her. Maybe it's because I wanted to kiss her earlier in the go-kart.

The same insecure song played in my head as I stared into her doe-brown eyes. *She doesn't want a fat boy, especially someone with a criminal record. She's way out of your league. Go date that girl from Waffle House Michael wanted you to meet.*

I shake my head and try to dislodge the thoughts that plague me every time I think of her that way—every time I've thought of any girl that way since my conviction.

Sadly, the fat-boy verse is a song as old as middle school. Everyone wanted to be friends with Earl Ed, but nobody wanted to date him.

"Is something wrong?"

"Huh?" I snap out of my momentary pity party to find Mackenzie staring at me.

"No. Just thinking . . ." I crank the truck and head out of the parking lot as if I weren't in deep thought.

We drive the few miles to G-Maw's house, making small talk about the show and my family. Whatever insecurities I have about myself pale in comparison with those brought on by my extended family. No non-local girl would go for someone attached to them.

Michael's as handsome as they get, and even he had to marry a pregnant casino cocktail waitress, thanks to his crazy mama.

When I turn onto our family road, a large Santa "ho-ho-hos" at the truck. It's as tall as Woody and Misty's trailer and wiggles slightly in the breeze. This addition still doesn't outshine the usual half-dozen pink flamingos with reindeer antlers on their heads. Instead of pulling the plastic Santa sleigh this year, Woody has them lined up in front of the massive new Santa. There's also a wooden nativity, candy canes, and enough lights to signal a fighter jet.

"Interesting decor." Mackenzie tilts her head toward Santa as we exit the truck.

"That's a new feature."

"Yeah, I didn't see it up when we went to Carla's the other day."

"No, like totally new. Last year the flamingos were pulling an appropriate-sized sleigh."

"Oh." Mackenzie backs up, then screams when a goat bleats behind her. She jumps into my arms and buries her face in my chest.

"It's okay." I wrap my arm around her back and try not to think of her as anything other than a girl scared by an animal. That was much easier to do a few days earlier when she sought my safety from the motel rat. Now that I know her, the attraction runs much deeper than her physical features.

She jerks her head up, and our faces are now dangerously close. "What is that?"

I back us away from the goat pen and set her feet on the ground. "G-Paw's goats."

Mackenzie glances toward the pen. "How can something that cute sound so horrid?"

"Ah, goats are nasty and sometimes mean. I think God made them cute so we wouldn't shoot them on the spot."

She grimaces and snuggles even closer to me. Without thinking, I stroke my hand up and down the small of her back. When she raises an eyebrow, I drop my hand and take a step back.

"We best get inside. Mama will be here soon."

Mackenzie clears her throat. "Yeah. I want to get footage of her entering with the cookies."

We walk toward the house, and I take another sip of my tea. It's almost gone, but its best if I drink water with my meal to fill up quicker. Nothing can cause a former fatty to backslide like a grandma's Christmas meal.

Mackenzie taps the edge of the carport with her boot. "Is this—"

"Astroturf."

Her eyes narrow as if she's trying to figure out why.

I palm the back of my neck. "I tossed some ice out of a cooler once, and G-Maw fell and broke her hip. Not my finest moment."

Mackenzie pats my arm. "That's an accident, not your fault."

"Yeah, well, it was enough to scare her into hiring these turf people from Tuscaloosa to come cover all her concrete."

She gives my arm a slight squeeze. We lock eyes for a second, and I smile.

"We're here!" Mama's voice rings out over Woody's creepy Santa.

I flinch, and Mackenzie drops her hand from my arm. Ziggy lifts his camera—hopefully for the first time.

"Good, can you film Carla bringing in the cookies?" she asks.

"On it." Ziggy turns to the two guys with him and instructs them on the big, fuzzy microphone and cords. He turns back to Mackenzie. "And we're rolling. Go with it."

She nudges Mama, urging her to enter first. Mama smooths her hair with her free hand, then opens the door. Ziggy follows, then the rest of us follow him.

By the time I make it inside, everyone is staring at the crew, except for G-Paw. He somehow slipped away. I'm not surprised, as he believes anything with a video recorder is tapped by the government—including cell phones.

While everyone else scans the entire film crew, Aunt Misty is focused on the camera. She pulls something from her cleavage, and I wince. If she tries to vape in the house again, Aunt Bea will have another heart attack.

I let out a breath of relief when she opens the tube and starts running red lipstick across her lips. She combs her fingernails through her hair, then struts toward us while placing the lipstick in her shirt.

Mama grits her teeth, then steps between Ziggy and Misty. "Cookie, Misty?"

Misty pulls her aside and stands square in front of the camera. "Whatcha filming, blondie?"

Ziggy glances at Mackenzie, as if asking for help.

She shrugs. "Go with it. This is reality TV."

Misty claps her hands and turns toward the family. "Oh, Woody. I always said we should get our own reality show!"

Those two might make it a week on *Redneck Island*, but that's still iffy.

Misty slings her head around and leans toward Ziggy. "If you only have room for one star, my hubby's fine with staying at home," she whispers before winking dramatically.

I roll my eyes. Misty tosses her hair and sashays back to Woody.

"Would anyone else like a cookie?" Mama steps closer to the family.

Liam stands and takes a cookie. Misty comes back next. But instead of taking a cookie, she picks up Taco and Belle. Not the fast food, but her and Woody's twin Chihuahuas. They're wearing Christmas sweaters identical to Woody's. Even sadder, he likely had them custom made.

Krystal stands with her baby in her arms. Although I've trained myself not to look at her chest, I do double-check that the baby isn't stuck to it. I don't know much about this show, but I'm certain they want to keep it family friendly.

She walks up to Dougy with her baby on her hip. "You look familiar."

Dougy shrugs.

"Where are you from?"

"Meridian, Mississippi."

Krystal snaps her fingers and bounces on her toes, nearly dropping little Colleen. "I knew it! I'm from the Delta, but I lived in Tupelo, then Tunica the last little while." She blows a kiss to Michael. "Until I met Michael, and he whisked me away to Alabama."

Michael's face lights up with his signature goofy smile as he waves to the camera. Ziggy pans the room, spending extra time on Taco and Belle.

I can't blame him. Aside from maybe Colleen, they are the cutest of our bunch. He's zooming in as one scratches behind the ear with a rear leg when a loud whistle calls all our attention toward the kitchen.

G-Paw stands in the doorway with his dentures in one hand, and two fingers in his puckered lips. We all stare in silence as he replaces his teeth and announces, "Suppertime. Earl, say the prayer so I can eat."

CHAPTER EIGHT

Earl Ed

While Daddy prays over the food, I silently pray he won't say anything that may lead all of network television to think we're gun-toting, Bible-thumping, four-wheel-driving rednecks.

We're actually all of those things, but it might not sit well for the show.

Daddy says "amen," and I sigh. We made it through one of his speech-prayers with only one mention of the Second Amendment. That must be a new record.

Woody removes his hand from his heart and salutes. I sincerely hope the camera didn't get that.

G-Maw shuffles toward the kitchen, spouting directions as to what is where. Mama takes the remainder of the cookies to the dessert table, which is a card table with a Christmas tablecloth. Aunt Robin follows her and begins filling red Solo cups with ice.

I hang back beside Mackenzie and watch G-Maw try and convince Ziggy that they should take a break and eat. He assures her he's used to eating last and that he's mastered eating with one hand while the camera is on a tripod.

"What kind of food should I expect?" Mackenzie cranes her neck, but can't see inside the kitchen yet.

"A little of this and a little of that. Home cooking."

"Sounds good. I don't get that often."

"Your family not cook?"

She balks. "It's just my mother and me, and no, we don't cook."

"So what do y'all eat on Christmas?"

She crosses her arms and stares at the wall ahead. "Mother is usually on some kind of trip. If I'm not working, I order Chinese."

My eyebrows draw together as I study her face for an emotion. The lack of sadness in her eyes proves this is normal for her. And that makes me sad.

"Well, tonight you can enjoy a full-blown family Christmas. Complete with crazy relatives and weird games."

She laughs. "I'm looking forward to it."

I smile at her as we cross the threshold into the small kitchen. G-Maw hands us both a plastic plate. They're the good kind, rectangular, with separate compartments to hold a little of everything.

We're halfway through the line when the front door shuts. All eyes turn to see who's here. Since the neighbors usually come in right before Dirty Santa, my money is on Paul. Nope, it's Bradley.

"Howdy, Mayberrys. Look what the cat drug in." He steps aside. My cousin Lacie enters, along with her new husband, Collins.

G-Maw pushes people twice her size out of the way to hug Lacie. Aunt Robin is next in line for a hug, then Woody.

Collins gives him some weird side-eye when he hugs Lacie a beat too long. As he should, since Woody had no business hugging her to begin with. I'm afraid Aunt Misty has rubbed off on him, rather than the other way around.

"Sorry we're late. We both worked this morning."

I nod toward the couple. "That's my cousin Lacie and her husband. They live in Atlanta."

Mackenzie nods. As I turn toward the dessert table, something shoves into my back.

Krystal rushes behind me, buttoning her shirt on her way to the living room. Another visual I can't unsee.

Woody's inappropriate hug for Lacie doesn't hold a candle to Krystal leaping on Collins. "Oh, my hero."

Mackenzie snaps her head my way. "What's that about?"

"You've got to see your little namesake once she wakes from her nap," Krystal spouts out.

If the baby is napping, why was her shirt undone? I shake my head. Not my problem. Instead, I focus on Mackenzie. "Collins delivered her baby last Christmas."

"Oh." Mackenzie's nose and lips unfurl, as if that makes it okay in her mind. "He's her doctor?"

"Technically no. But he's a doctor, and he delivered her baby when she went into labor."

Her nose wrinkles again. "So he used to work here?"

I laugh. "Nope. She went into labor at our hog killing."

Mackenzie drops the pig-butt cookie she's holding and selects a reindeer instead. "And I'm done asking questions."

I smirk. "Wise woman."

The rest of the meal goes smoother because I manage to keep us a safe distance from Aunt Misty, Woody, and Krystal —the trifecta that could shame our family on TV. We finish our meal in the den while G-Maw and Lacie organize all the gifts.

CRAZY RICH REDNECKS

"You said you brought me a gift?" Mackenzie whispers in my ear.

Her breath tickles the side of my face, and I get a whiff of her scent. It's something flowery, and I restrain myself from sucking it in like a dog sniffing out a coon. She's witnessed enough creepiness from the terrifying trio tonight.

"Yeah, I keep gift cards on hand."

"Thanks." We share a smile that's quickly interrupted by Woody screaming.

"I have an announcement!" He stands and attempts to beat a plastic fork against a red Solo cup. Instead of making a sound, it sloshes tea on G-Maw's white tablecloth.

He sets down the cup, and Aunt Robin rushes over with some napkins. Undeterred by the mess, Woody continues. "I brought each family a gift to celebrate my good fortune this Christmas."

Everyone exchanges glances as we gather near Woody. Without any explanation, he walks out the front door. Some watch him go toward his trailer, while the rest of us continue eating and talking.

A few minutes later, the door opens to Woody rolling a huge Yeti cooler. "My ex gave Misty and me full custody of Taco and Belle, so to celebrate, I smoked a bunch of butts!"

He throws back the cooler lid and takes out multiple Dollar General bags filled with Boston butts, handing one to the head of every family. When he gets to me, his eyes widen. "Gosh, I didn't know the camera people would be here."

"It's fine. We don't need one," Mackenzie answers.

Woody's face falls. Mackenzie slants her eyes at me, then back at him. "It's okay, really. I'm part Jewish."

I bite the inside of my jaw to keep from laughing. I've seen her eat bacon several times.

Woody cocks his head, not making the connection. Then

his jaw drops. "Oh, ma'am, I do apologize for the nativity on my lawn."

Mackenzie blushes, and a slight laugh sneaks out of me. "No, it's fine, I promise," she says sheepishly.

Woody takes the butt from my arms and shoves it toward Mackenzie. "I insist. Take Earl Ed's and feed your people." Then he looks at me. "I would give her mine, but the kids like it too much." He points to Taco or Belle—I'm not sure which—chewing on a bone by the kitchen table.

"Dirty Santa time!" G-Maw shuffles around, shaking a red Solo cup. "Draw a number and find a seat."

Ziggy follows G-Maw with the camera as she lets everyone draw numbers.

Once we're all in the den, Mackenzie scans the room. "Were all these people here before?"

"No. Some are neighbors from the next road over, and you've met Paul and Ms. Dot."

She nods, then turns to Ziggy. "We need to shoot B-roll only for this. I don't think the boom mic will fit in here with so many people."

"Got it." Ziggy says something to the other guys, who happily put down their equipment and go fix plates.

Daddy stands up and announces the rules to the game as he does every year. And someone questions them, as they do every year. That leads to a short discussion about whether the number one rule is fair or not. Finally, we get to play.

Bradley is first and opens an envelope. Inside is a two-dollar bill. He holds it up for everyone to see.

"Check the package, Bradley, there's gotta be more than that. We always spend ten," I say.

He holds up the open envelope. "That's all, big dog. Nowhere to hide anything in this."

Mackenzie opens her mouth to say something, then stops. I can see the confusion on her face.

I lean closer and whisper, "We have a ten-dollar spending cap."

She nods.

Krystal giggles. "That's a good gift. It's worth at least ten dollars."

A few people shoot her "bless her heart" stares. Liam point-blank says what we're all thinking. "No, it's worth two dollars, like it says."

Krystal's smile fades and her eyes widen. She turns to Michael, who pats her leg sympathetically. Then she turns to Bradley. "At the casinos, some people would tip us with those. My coworker would always trade me hers for a five-dollar bill, saying they were worth at least ten."

Bradley shakes his head, as muffled moans echo around the room. "Sorry, Krystal. Sounds like you got screwed out of three dollars."

She pokes out her bottom lip and lowers her head. Michael kisses her hair and wraps an arm around her.

Bradley stands to break the tension and holds up the two-dollar bill. "Okay, who's got number two?"

We go around the room, opening our fair share of flashlights and candles. It's safe to say we'll be set if the power goes out.

Ziggy zooms in when Aunt Bea reaches for Mama's gift. She opens the tin and frowns. "Cookies. We just ate cookies. I want a gift."

The room goes silent, and Mackenzie slides her hand over her throat, signaling Ziggy to cut the camera. He does so and retreats to the kitchen to eat with the other guys.

Daddy is next and opens one of my gifts. He puts on his reading glasses. "Ten dollars to Double Drive." He stares at me over the rim of his readers. "Son, if I want to ride a go-kart, I'll just go there."

"And now you won't have to pay." I fold my arms and grin.

Daddy sits down and tucks the card in his shirt pocket. He mumbles something, and by the look on his face, I'm glad the camera is off.

Liam is the last to open a gift and goes for a flat rectangular package in the corner. He must know what it is, or else he'd steal his dad's Tractor Supply gift card.

He jerks the wrapping off and holds up a green road sign that reads, "Mayberry Road."

"That's where that went!" G-Paw jumps to his feet and scowls. "I've been looking for that all week."

Liam drops the sign in his lap and holds up his palms. "I swear, G-Paw, I didn't pull it down. It was on the ground when I got it."

G-Paw leaves the room as usual. Liam smiles down at his sign, then straightens his face when he makes eye contact with his father.

"Okay, is that all the numbers?" Daddy asks.

Nods and yeses fill the room. "Number one, your pick."

"Not fair," one of the neighbor kids spouts off. His mom shushes him.

Bradley walks over to Liam and holds out the two-dollar bill. "I'll take the sign, please."

Liam sighs and snatches the money, then hands Bradley the sign. "Fine."

Bradley tucks the sign under his arm and laughs. "Been a pleasure, Mayberry family, but I best get back to my patrol." He tips his cowboy hat and starts toward the door.

G-Maw stops him. "Thanks for getting the sign, Bradley. How soon do you think it will be back on the road?"

Bradley shrugs. "That depends on when the county can make a new one. This one's going in my office."

I turn to Mackenzie. "And that is why we call it Dirty Santa."

Mackenzie

I set the Boston butt and my Dirty Santa gift on the counter in Double Drive's kitchen. Earl Ed retrieves a knife and some plates, while the hungry crew gathers nearby in booths.

Earl Ed tends to the butt as I sniff my candle. "Not bad. Very fruity."

He peers over his shoulder. "Yeah, that's a G-Maw gift. She's big on candles."

"I prefer that to a flashlight."

"Or a Double Drive coupon."

I laugh. "I'd use it for mini golf. I need a break from go-kart driving."

"But you're such a natural." Earl Ed winks.

I smile, my cheeks warming at our easy banter. I'll miss him once filming wraps. When it comes to staying with someone easy to talk to and hospitable, he outshines all the fancy concierge people in New York.

"Hey, Mackenzie." Ziggy rushes in with a smile that spreads ear to ear. "I got some great footage tonight." He turns to Earl Ed. "Man, your family is a riot."

"Oh, Lord, help us."

"No, man. Your bunch will be famous."

I hold up a hand. "Ziggy, dial it down a notch. Remember, this show is about Carla and her cookies, not the family."

Ziggy drops his shoulders. "I know." Then he perks up a bit. "But if the network ever wants a spin off . . ."

I take a plate of barbecue and shove it at his chest. "Go enjoy your after-dinner snack."

Ziggy mopes toward the snack area like a teenager who's been given a strict curfew.

"Thanks." Earl Ed smiles at me when Ziggy disappears behind the wall.

"For what?"

He plates more barbecue, then wraps up what's left of the butt. "For not letting him totally humiliate us on TV."

I laugh. "I can't make any promises, but I'll try."

Voices echo from the opposite end of the building. I stick my head in the main room. All the guys are laughing and talking as they eat in the booths. But there's a more singsongy sound coming from the front.

"What's that?"

Earl Ed lifts the bag of pork remains. "The scraps. I'll feed them to Uncle Joey's dog tomorrow. I cut all good stuff off for the guys."

"Shhh, no listen," I whisper. "Either I'm hearing things or someone is singing 'Deck the Halls.'"

Earl Ed rolls his eyes. He washes his hands and joins me by the doorway. "If we ignore them long enough, maybe they'll go away."

"Who?"

"Carolers."

"Like the singing Christmas song people in movies?"

"Yeah, except they're on my porch, making stray dogs howl."

"I didn't hear a dog howl."

Earl Ed lifts a finger. "Wait for it . . ."

Someone hits a high note and a dog belts out in the distance.

"Huh, how'd you know?"

"This happens every year. Of course, I haven't been here a year yet, but they travel county-wide."

Curiosity gets the best of me, and I start toward the front entrance.

"Mackenzie, what are you doing?"

Before Earl Ed can catch up to me, I open the door. At least a dozen people dressed like the cast of *Scrooge* stare back at me. They sing the last leg of the song in unison. I've never been much of a Christmas music fan, but this is starting to grow on me.

It's refreshing to see people dressed like this, caroling to neighbors, when it isn't part of a staged production.

Once the song ends, they smile at me and cheer, "Merry Christmas!"

I applaud them, then notice Carla among the mix. "Carla, why didn't you tell me you were caroling tonight?"

"We didn't think this needed filming. It's just something we do every year to get people in the Christmas spirit."

Misty pushes through the crowd. "Speak for yourself, Carla. This could be my big break." She bats fake eyelashes at me.

I scan her wardrobe, which is way more saloon girl than Victorian. She slings her hair over her shoulder and starts belting out something about a hard candy Christmas.

Nobody backs her up, except for the stray dog in the distance.

A slurping sound catches my attention, and I turn to several of the crew members standing behind us. Dougy sucks down his drink and grins. Misty has captivated at least one audience member.

"I'll volunteer to take the camera." Dougy's eyes widen with anticipation.

I turn to Carla. "Are you okay with me tagging along for some B-roll?"

She nods. "I actually have some cookies in my SUV for when we sing at the hospital."

I look at Earl Ed.

He scratches his beard. "I can drive you and Dougy behind them."

"Yes." Dougy does the cha-ching motion with his arm. "Let me get the good camera."

Before I can grab my purse and notebook, Dougy is back with the camera. We follow the carolers down the front steps. Earl Ed trails a few minutes behind as he tells the crew to lock up if they leave before we return.

I hesitate by the truck, before I realize I've grown accustomed to Earl Ed opening my door. After Dougy hops in the back, I get in, too. Earl Ed gets in a minute later and drives behind the van full of carolers.

The back of the vehicle reads "Wisteria Worship Center" in big block letters. I read it out loud.

"That's our church," Earl Ed comments.

"All these singers are from your church?"

"Except for Misty and Woody. They're more like Chreasters."

"What?" I wrinkle my forehead.

"Christmas and Easter Christians."

"Again, what?" That didn't exactly answer my question.

"They normally only attend church on Christmas and Easter."

"Hmm. Kind of like how some people only travel in the summer?"

"No, nothing like that."

I waver my head.

"It's a shame. Misty has such a great voice, I think she

should sing every Sunday." Dougy talks through a lovestruck smile.

Earl Ed and I both turn to him.

"What, you don't agree?"

We share a look, then face forward. After a few miles, the van turns at a traffic light. Almost immediately, we come to a sign welcoming us to Apple Cart, Alabama. I recognize Mary's and Piggly Wiggly before we turn again and park in front of a hospital.

The church van door slides open, and Woody hops out first. My guess is Misty picked out his costume as well because he's dressed as a Confederate soldier.

"Dougy, try not to get any close-up shots of Woody. That might paint the wrong picture."

"Got it."

We climb out of the truck and follow the group to the hospital entrance. Carla has a festive bag draped over her arm. She leads the crowd through the revolving door, which is somewhat of a challenge for Dougy. I take the camera before he drops it.

"Here." I hand it to him once he's in the lobby and standing steady.

"Thanks."

"Oh, hey. We've been expecting y'all." The woman at the front desk beams as she picks up a phone. "Dr. West, they're here," she speaks into the receiver.

A handsome young man in a white coat, along with other people wearing scrubs, appear in the lobby from every direction. Some are pushing patients in wheelchairs.

The carolers sing "We Wish You A Merry Christmas" as Carla passes out goody bags of cookies.

A little girl lingers near the tree in the center of the lobby. She isn't wearing pajamas, so she must be a visitor. I cross the room and bend in front of her.

"Hi."

She lifts one corner of her mouth. "Hi."

"Do you have family in the hospital?"

She shakes her head. "I'm waiting for my mama to get off work."

"Oh." I glance at the group of people in scrubs and white coats. "Is she a nurse or doctor?"

She shakes her head. "She's cleaning." The girl turns toward the hallway, where a woman is rolling a large trash can toward the exit. "She works at nighttime."

"Okay." I grin and bite my tongue. My guts says it's best not to ask about her dad.

"Would you like some Christmas cookies?"

She smiles widely, revealing a missing front tooth.

"Be right back." I rush to Carla. "Can I have a bag for someone?"

She smiles and nods, while continuing to sing.

I retrieve a bag and take it to the little girl. She grins wider and pulls out the cookies. "Thanks. I'll save the snowman for Mama."

My heart aches. I hug her on impulse. She wraps her willowy arms around my neck and whispers, "Merry Christmas."

I hold her for a long moment and suck in a breath. I've never been a crier, but it takes all I have to not break down. I want to tell her it will all be okay when she gets older. That I can relate to her life.

But I can't promise that. All this Christmas togetherness —for real, not Hallmark—has me questioning the lack of family in my own life.

CHAPTER NINE

Earl Ed

I yawn as Mama goes over the details for a Santa cowboy cookie. She can call it a Santa all she wants, but to me it looks like Bradley with a beard.

She packs it in a container on top of a pile of other cookies, then closes the lid and smiles at the camera.

"And cut." Mackenzie claps her hands. "Nice work, Carla. I love cowboy Santa."

"Thanks, dear."

That's my cue to fill a bottle of ice water without anyone scolding me for interfering with the sound. I open the drawer to the ice maker. After I started Double Drive, Daddy had this installed to get the same small-pellet ice I have.

He swears it's because he got addicted to my ice. However, he's always trying to one-up me. I wouldn't put it past him to install a fountain machine in the basement or add a golf course to the backyard. For all I know, he may have already tried and gotten blocked by Mama.

Mackenzie walks toward the cookies. "Do you want me to go ahead and load them before we start the next batch?"

"Oh no, they will stay here."

Mackenzie wrinkles her forehead at Mama. "But we're going to your sister-in-law's house, right?"

"Yeah, then to G-Maw's, then back here."

Mackenzie cocks her head to the side, then thumbs through her notes.

"It's a progressive dinner," I chime in as I add water to my coveted rat-turd ice.

"Yeah, I wrote that down. Three courses. But it says we go to Robin and Joey's house."

I laugh. "We do, then progress to G-Maw's for the main course, then progress back over here for desserts." I emphasize the word "progress" each time.

"Interesting. I assumed progressive meant something else entirely." Mackenzie closes her notebook.

"And on that note, I'm gone." I slap a hat on my head and turn to leave.

"Where are you going?"

I open my mouth to answer Mackenzie, when Daddy steps beside me with a rifle. She arches a brow at the massive gun.

"To shoot things," I say.

Mama grins. "Oh, take the boys some of these." She opens a plastic bowl and pulls out some Christmas tree cookies.

Daddy takes them, then kisses her on the cheek. Ziggy raises the camera and steps closer to them.

Daddy shoves him against the cabinets by the camera. "Not filming me, son." He drops his hand from the camera and pats Ziggy's shoulder. "Gotta draw the line somewhere."

He turns, takes his gun, and walks out, head held high. I wink at Mackenzie and try not to laugh at her shocked expression. Then I follow Daddy outside.

"What you packing, son?"

"My good buddies, Smith and Wesson."

I stop by my truck for the gun and ammo, then get in with him. Numerous guns line the back seat and floorboard of his truck. One in particular catches my eye. It was G-Paw's dad's gun, and it rarely leaves Daddy's gun room.

"What's G-Daddy's rifle doing in here?"

"Oh, I'm thinking of giving it to Michael."

The blood drains from my face. Daddy hasn't had it that long, and G-Paw passed it to him as his only son. Shouldn't he save it for *me*?

"Why Michael?"

"So it can keep going through generations. He has a family now."

I clinch my fists, trying to calm down before I unload on Daddy. Verbally, of course, not with the guns.

A few miles pass before I'm no longer tingling and can control my voice. "Wouldn't you want to pass it on to our branch of the family?"

"Well, yeah, but you don't have any kids."

"Not yet."

Daddy chuckles, offending me more—if that's even possible.

"What's so funny?"

We turn down the dirt road to Gamer's Paradise, and I pray he hits a huge mud hole with his new truck.

"You're not exactly close to getting married, and your sister's still young. God only knows what she'll marry." His eyes narrow, and his knuckles whiten against the steering wheel. No doubt, he's worrying about his future son-in-law already.

So now we're both mad. Great!

I swallow and decide now's as good a time as any to discuss this. "So you're assuming Carly will marry some tool who can't shoot a gun, and I'll never marry or have kids?"

We park near the massive dirt target where we shoot every Christmas Eve. He cuts the engine and faces me. "Sad to say, but that's exactly what I'm assuming."

I stare out the windshield and pout like a puppy passed over at the pound. That may be the answer I anticipated, but it still stings. Daddy gets out and collects his portable arsenal. I wait until he's at the tailgate to get out with my one measly gun. The one he gave me the day I got out of jail.

Is it a great gun? Yes. But from a man who owns over a hundred, it doesn't mean that much. Especially when he earmarks the most sentimental gun in the family for my cousin.

If Michael weren't such a good friend, I'd have every right to disown him. Daddy's always favored him over me, long before I got arrested.

I'm loading my gun when Michael walks up. Impeccable timing, cuz.

Colleen is strapped to the front of him in one of those baby-carrying pouches. She's wearing camouflage like the rest of us, and some of those noise-canceling earmuffs.

"Hey, cuz." He nods at my hand. "I see you brought the Smith and Wesson."

"And I see you brought a baby . . . to a gun range."

He grins. "Krystal's busy fixing her food for the dinner tonight."

"Yes, I can imagine it takes a while for Viennas to marinate in Cheez Whiz."

Michael's grin fades slightly, and he blinks, as if contemplating whether that was a burn or serious statement. And this is the family Daddy wants to give a gun?

I sigh and take my gun to the opposite side of the dirt pile. Bradley tips that dumb hat at me. "Afternoon, Earl Ed."

"Officer." I focus on the dirt pile and contemplate in what world have I chosen the company of Bradley over Michael.

Uncle Joey drives up with Liam and Collins, and they start unloading guns. They have a lot, but not as much as Daddy.

He brought more than we can shoot in the time we have, but I think that's his way of showing off. As president of the Alabama Gun Club three years running, he likes to remind everyone of his gun knowledge and ownership.

Jack goes to the dirt and points to the Christmas tree shape spray painted in the center. Inside the tree are red dots of various sizes. He explains how many points each size dot is worth, then ends with, "Good luck."

When he nods and steps back, I halfway regret not bringing Ziggy. This would make for a fun mini-segment, similar to an amateur *Top Shot*—Christmas edition.

As usual, Bradley volunteers to go first. Daddy offers to shoot against him. I hang back by the truck while several shooters compete, happy to stay in my own little world. I'm still a little rusty after not having shot much in the past decade.

"Earl Ed, you want to go against Michael?"

I lift my head to Jack, along with everyone else, waiting on my response. "Uh, sure."

I slide off the tailgate and get my gun. Michael is in front of the dirt pile, still wearing Colleen on his chest. I cross my arms. "Give the baby to someone. That's just insane."

"If it makes you more comfortable."

I roll my eyes. Michael frowns, but he unhooks the baby pouch and hands her to Collins. The good doctor has enough sense to walk toward the lodge, taking her farther from our obnoxious shooting.

Daddy must not care for me snapping at Michael, because he walks over with *the* gun. "Here, son, use this one."

Even Uncle Joey gasps when he hands the gun to Michael instead of me. Of all the low, dirty . . .

"Thanks." Michael hands Daddy his newer, unsentimental rifle.

"Why don't you go first?" I say.

"Thanks." Clueless Michael steps forward and squares his shoulders. He makes a decent shot, but hits one of the easier targets.

I step up, my palms sweaty and shaking. Despite having a successful practice last week and becoming a bit of a paintball-gun pro, I'm nervous. I say a quick prayer and fire my pistol. To my amazement, it hits the best target.

Everyone cheers, and Jack reminds us of the score. Again, he'd make a great amateur *Top Shot* host.

The second round, I'm still ahead. I smile, then straighten my face when I spot Daddy scowling from a short distance. That's all it takes for me to do something stupid.

"How about the winner gets G-Daddy's gun?"

Nobody says a word. You could hear a mouse peeing on cotton a mile away. This bunch is well acquainted with the history of that rifle and what it means to my family. Even Liam shakes his head, signaling I've made a huge mistake.

Michael, ignorant to the rift between Daddy and me, steps up and shoots. He hits one of the better targets. Still, the only way he can beat me is if I totally screw up.

I glance around the crowd. Daddy is nowhere to be found. He could just be peeing behind a truck door, but the fact that he isn't watching this hurts me more than him wanting to give Michael the gun.

I take a deep breath and fire my last bullet at the ground

in front of the dirt pile, solidifying Michael as the winner. Then I hold out my hand to him.

"Congratulations."

Being the airhead he is, he grins and shakes my hand. "You were great 'til the end. Good job, buddy."

"Yeah, buddy." That comes out laced with sarcasm, but I can no longer hide my jealousy.

I secure my gun and go back to the truck. Then I walk until I get cell service and text Mama to see if she or Carly can come pick me up. I'm done with this father-son bonding crap.

Mackenzie

Carla meets us at her sister-in-law's house, which is almost exactly between her house and G-Maw's. I try and focus on directing Ziggy, but my mind drifts to Earl Ed.

He called Carla about something before we left her house, and the tone of her voice and furrow of her brow concerned me. It's the first time she's been anything but all smiles. Surely she would've said something to us if he were in trouble.

I do my best to push the matter aside and follow Carla to Robin's house. The inside is the epitome of a Hallmark movie. It's a log cabin with a real wood-burning fireplace. A large Christmas tree stands on one side of the room beside a piano.

The entire decor is Christmas, from throw blankets to pillows, to garland around the entryways. Similar to Carla's all-out decor, but in a much cozier, more homey sense. I like it, especially since it's real and not a movie set.

Robin rushes in from the kitchen with her sleeves rolled up. "Welcome, come on in, y'all."

She loops her arm through mine and leads us to the kitchen, which continues the homey Christmas theme. Only the tree in this room is decorated with tractors. Lacie turns and greets us from the sink, where she's washing dishes.

"Make yourselves at home, and set up wherever you like." Robin unloops her arm from mine and fans her hand around the kitchen. "Everyone will come through here to fix plates, then mingle throughout the house."

Ziggy scans the area for outlets and points out a few places that he thinks would work well to shoot. As we're discussing camera angles for interviews, Earl Ed walks in. He's still wearing camo, along with that stupid Eddie hat. His face screams stressed.

Carla hugs him and whispers something.

"No, do not talk to him. I'm fine," he snaps back.

I'm not sure what happened, but he is clearly not fine.

"Mackenzie, what do you think of adjacent to the living room tree for the interviews?"

I turn from Earl Ed to Ziggy. "That's good. I think we can get the tree in the background."

"Yep." Ziggy heads for the living room, and I follow. Every time I try and sneak to the kitchen to talk with Earl Ed, someone on the crew asks me something insignificant.

Not that lighting and sound are considered insignificant in our business, but they are compared to whatever is concerning Earl Ed.

We finally agree on a setup, and I slide past Rambo's boom mic to find Earl Ed. That's when the doorbell rings. Ziggy pans the camera toward Robin and Joey, who open the door.

At least twenty people file inside carrying dishes and plates and Crock-Pots. If Carla hadn't explained how this works, I'd assume someone died.

Ziggy follows Robin until she gets to Carla, who he then zooms in on. This should be an easy night for the guys, mostly shooting B-roll and eating for free.

I sit on the piano bench to stay out of the crowd and find interesting people to interview. Paul stands out, mainly for his shiny belt buckle and bright red-and-green-checkered shirt. He's holding a Styrofoam box, which makes me wonder what he brought.

Earl Ed sneaks past and opens the front door. The crew is busy filming people in the kitchen, so I go out behind him.

"Earl Ed?"

He turns and almost drops what looks like a stuffed jalapeño. "Hey, Mackenzie."

I cross the front porch and sit in the rocking chair beside him. "I hope you don't mind me asking, but are you okay?"

"Yeah." He pops the pepper in his mouth and faces the front lawn.

A massive dog comes out of the shadows and climbs the porch steps. I pick up my feet in case he bites.

"Hey, Bully." Earl Ed holds out his hand, and the dog sucks to him like Misty to a camera lens. He pets the beast and says something in a sappy voice I can't understand. Bully lies down in front of Earl Ed and snorts.

I slowly lower my feet, convinced he's harmless. "Did you have fun hunting?" Might as well strike up a casual conversation.

"We didn't hunt. We just shot."

"At what?" I can't imagine why anyone would shoot just to shoot.

"A Christmas tree."

I raise my eyebrows, and Earl Ed laughs a little. Seeing him not so down lessens my worry.

"It was a dirt bank spray painted like a tree with ornament targets."

I wrinkle my nose, trying to imagine how they hang ornaments on dirt. Hunters are strange. Even when they're not hunting.

Earl Ed bites into another jalapeño and rocks in his chair. The wind picks up, and I rub my thinly sleeved arms at the sudden chill. It's been so mild here that I haven't bothered to wear a jacket.

"Here." Earl Ed stands and drapes a camouflage coat around my shoulders.

"Thanks." I pull my arms through the sleeves and zip it. "This is surprisingly comfortable."

He nods. "And it goes with your black-and-brown color scheme."

"Haha."

He laughs, and I smile at his mood lifting. I'd like to think I had something to do with that, even if it's at the expense of laughing at me.

The front door opens, and Paul struts out, carrying the same Styrofoam box as before, plus two paper plates covered in tinfoil. He slides the toothpick in his mouth to the side and greets us. We mumble hellos, then he jogs down the front steps, awfully spry for an older man.

"Do you know what he brought?"

Earl Ed balks. "Ms. Dot."

"No, I mean as an appetizer."

"Exactly."

I roll my eyes. "Don't be crude."

"I'm not. I mean he never brings food, only leaves with it."

"Doesn't that go against all this Southern hospitality?"

"Exactly."

Paul appears from the shadows and jogs up the steps, toothpick now square-center in his mouth. He goes inside and returns a minute later with Ms. Dot on his arm.

"See you kids at the next stop," Ms. Dot calls as she shuffles toward the steps.

Michael's family steps onto the porch next. The baby grins at me, and my heart skips a beat. Weird, since I've never wanted a baby . . . like not ever, not even a little.

Krystal balances the baby on one hip and a baking dish on the other. "Any of y'all want some seven-layer dip?" She lifts the dish slightly.

"No thank you," I say.

"Earl Ed?" She wiggles her thinly plucked eyebrows.

"No thanks."

Michael lifts his chin at Earl Ed, then takes the baby from Krystal. He continues down the steps without saying a word. I suspect this may have something to do with Earl Ed's mood. Krystal follows him with the dish.

Earl Ed waits until they're gone to comment. "About four of those seven layers are Cheez Whiz."

"What's that?"

"Exactly."

The door opens to Ziggy with the camera. "I think we've got everything we need here. Carla said we can head to G-Maw's anytime we want."

I glance at Earl Ed, who's petting the massive dog. He seems okay now.

"I'm ready when you are," I say to Ziggy.

As much as I want to stay and unpeel the layers of Earl Ed to make sure he's really okay, it's none of my business. Besides, the number-one rule in my business is staying out of drama concerning the cast and crew. I imagine my temporary landlord/Uber driver fits into that category as well.

CHAPTER TEN

Earl Ed

I resist the urge to eat my weight in deer poppers, even if they are keto-friendly. It's not Michael's fault Daddy's always favored him. Still, it doesn't make being around him any easier after today.

"Earl Ed, can you help us with the tea?"

"Yes, ma'am," I call to Aunt Robin.

I stand from my seat on the couch beside Liam. Everyone but family is leaving to prepare for the next destination—G-Maw's house.

Aunt Robin has the entire kitchen island covered with jugs of sweet tea. Every year, she volunteers to bring the tea to G-Maw's to save the entire community from sugar overload. G-Maw has shown no sign of catching on to why someone would offer to buy twenty jugs of tea when she's more than willing to make it. Of course, if anyone can get away with doing something out of the kindness of their heart—real or fake—it would be Aunt Robin.

"Liam, come in here." Even though he's not on the clock at Double Drive, I can get more out of him than anyone else around here.

He slugs into the kitchen.

"Help us load your mama's tea in my truck."

He sighs, but arms up several bottles and heads for the front door. I carry more behind him as Aunt Robin rushes to open the door for us.

We somehow make it down the front steps without tripping and then across the yard. My truck is parked in the dark, which adds a bit of a challenge. Unlike Mama's decorations, Aunt Robin's stop at the front door.

I've almost made it to the bed of the truck when my knees hit something and send me tumbling forward. Bully howls and growls at the same time, which is a bit impressive. Sweet tea flies across the grass, one bottle bursting on impact.

"Way to go," Liam comments.

I curse him under my breath and wobble to my feet. "Help me get this up."

He sets his jugs in the truck, then helps gather mine. "None of these have holes."

"Good." I pick up the empty bottle with a crack in the side. "I'll throw this one away inside. Open my truck door for light, and we'll get the rest."

I pet Bully as a peace offering. It takes him a minute, but he wags his tail and licks the tea-soiled grass. I sneak the empty jug in the trash can to not worry Aunt Robin. Then we gather the rest and pack them in the truck.

"Want to ride over with me?"

Liam shakes his head. "I'm gonna take my truck in case any hot girls are there."

"Suit yourself."

I drive to the end of our road and park in the ditch near Woody's Santa. Everyone takes up the field next to G-Maw's house, but it's worth dodging a few goats to ensure nobody's blocking me in. Liam pulls up behind me. So much for that.

At least he's handy to carry in the tea. We don't have to worry about blind spots in G-Maw's yard, thanks to Woody's winter wonderland behind us.

We arm up the tea and head toward the house.

Ziggy has the camera set up on the porch, and I immediately scan the yard for Mackenzie. I was distracted when she talked to me at Aunt Robin's and want to make up for it.

"Hey, guys." I greet Ziggy and Rambo as I cross the Astroturf.

"Dude, your grandma's fake grass would make a sick green screen."

"I don't know what that means . . . but thanks?"

"Need help with those?" Rambo takes all my tea with one arm, and all Liam's with the other.

"Thanks. Take them to the kitchen."

He nods and somehow manages to open the door with the toe of his boot. Impressive.

Liam and I go back for the rest and take it inside. I see the back of Mackenzie's head across the kitchen.

G-Paw whistles to get everyone's attention. Then G-Maw steps forward and announces, "Now that the drinks are here, we can eat. We have chicken and dumplings, or dumplings and chicken." She pauses for everyone to laugh at her humorless joke. At this point, we laugh more to appease her. "And biscuits."

Several people have already formed a line in front of the dumplings, with Paul at the front.

"So all these massive pots are dumplings?"

I turn and smile at Mackenzie behind me. "Yep."

"Why all dumplings?"

"G-Maw makes the best in the county. She said it would be a shame to deprive anyone of hers."

Mackenzie laughs. "I can't decide if that's really sweet or really conceited."

"Both." I grin as she laughs harder.

We fall in line behind the others, and I strike up a conversation to hopefully make up for my sour mood at Joey and Robin's house.

"Did y'all get some good footage at Aunt Robin's?"

"Yeah. Her decorations are great."

"Her house has always been my favorite. I used to hang out there a lot as a kid because she'd let us eat macaroni in the living room."

Mackenzie snickers. "And Carla wouldn't?"

"What do you think?"

She shrugs. "My mom was a costume designer. We ate most of our meals in the living room while she adjusted clothing for the next day's call time."

I stare at the floor so she won't see the pity on my face. Aside from the decade I spent in confinement, my family ate all our meals around the table together. Even then, Mama would bring me a picnic lunch to eat in the visitor's room with them.

Mackenzie hands me a plastic bowl, and I scoop it full of dumplings. I skip a biscuit since I want to enjoy a dessert later. One of the church women always makes her famous cookie crack cake.

"Is that a wig?"

I turn in the direction Mackenzie is looking and spot Aunt Misty in her full Dolly Parton attire. "I'm afraid so."

Mackenzie cocks her head and studies Misty. "Is she caroling again?"

"Something to that effect." I grab some napkins and leave the line before Misty sees us.

I'm almost positive she's been somewhere impersonating Dolly Parton. My guess is the nursing home, since they're her only repeat customers, and because her wig smells like mildew.

"Come on." In a pinch to escape Aunt Misty, I grab Mackenzie's hand and lead her toward the den.

My nerves flare as we rush through the crowd, hand in hand. For a spilt second, I pretend we're an actual couple seeking alone time, rather than two near strangers seeking solitude from my aunt's Dolly Parton impersonation. Once we make it to the den, I drop her hand, making mine go numb. She stares at me with flushed cheeks.

"A total waste!" G-Paw yells from the corner of the room, drawing my attention away from her.

He kicks the giant Saran Wrap ball like a star punter. I duck as it flies past our heads and lands in a bowl of scented leaves on the piano lid.

Mackenzie's eyes widen as she watches the ball roll onto the floor. "Who plays the piano in your family?"

"Nobody."

She raises a brow. "Then why do you all have pianos?"

I shrug. "Everyone over forty in the South owns a piano."

"Strange."

G-Paw brushes past us, muttering something under his breath.

Mackenzie turns to me. "What's his deal with that ball?"

"He thinks Saran Wrap is a precious commodity since it was rare when he was younger."

We eat a few minutes in silence, then singing echoes from the other room. I almost choke on my dumplings when Daddy yells, "Cut it out, Misty. This ain't the firemen's lodge or old folks' home."

Aunt Misty sticks her nose in the air and stomps off so hard that her pink cowgirl boots can be heard against the carpeted floor. I watch until her coat of many colors disappears behind G-Maw's fiber-optic Christmas tree.

"Gather around," G-Maw shouts from the kitchen.

I savor my last spoonful of dumplings and look at Mackenzie. She stands and meets Ziggy in the doorway between the kitchen and den. They find a spot for him to stand with the camera. Mackenzie scoots beside me as people crowd into the den. I set my empty bowl on the nearest end table, which is overtaken by a Christmas village display, complete with cotton snow.

G-Maw stands in the center of the room with the massive, wrapped ball. "Everyone unwraps one layer, then passes the ball. If a prize falls out on your turn, you can keep it."

She rolls the ball toward the recliner, and it hits a foot. I follow the Air Jordans up to athletic pants, a Braves jersey, and a gold chain. Surely not.

Yep. It's Jeffrey, one of Misty's ex-husbands. Every time they swap their kids on a holiday, he hangs around to get a gift. I should've known if he wasn't here for Dirty Santa, he'd come for this.

He digs his fingertips into the Saran Wrap and pulls back what has to be serval layers until a two-dollar bill hits the floor. It's likely the same two-dollar bill from Dirty Santa.

Jeffrey holds it up and smiles. "Cool. I've never seen one of these."

I try and make eye contact with Mackenzie, but she's focused on the ball rolling across the floor. Her face shines like a kid waiting on Santa. My chest tightens at seeing the joy on her face.

All these traditions are pretty whack to me, but I easily forget how much they mean to someone who doesn't get to spend their holidays with a big, crazy family.

Mackenzie

When all the guests head for their cars, Lacie and Collins gather the leftover tea in G-Maw's kitchen.

"Let me help with that." I reach for a bottle, but Lacie puts a hand on my arm.

"It's fine. We got it. They're just going to the basement refrigerator."

"Well, I don't mind—"

"Trust me." Collins stares at me with wild eyes, like someone who's outran a serial killer and wants to warn everyone around. "You're not ready for what's down there."

"Okay . . ." I tiptoe away from the kitchen and find my film crew.

Dougy is packing up equipment, so I stop and help roll up one of the extension cords. Ziggy and Rambo have one camera and the boom mic still running to interview the man in the Braves jersey.

Five minutes of hearing him talk, and I already don't like the guy. For the record, it has nothing to do with me being a Mets fan.

"So you were once married to Misty?" Ziggy asks.

"Yeah." He shakes his head. "Longest ten months of my life."

"Ten months? I thought you had two kids with her."

"I do." He holds up the two-dollar bill he unraveled from the Saran Wrap. "First one to hit a homer tomorrow gets this baby."

"Uh, you play ball on Christmas?"

"Yeah, it's the Christmas Classic."

Earl Ed walks past us, and I stuff the extension cord in a bag. I motion to Rambo that I'm going with Earl Ed and escape outside from baseball dad. I may work on Christmas, but at least I don't force kids to skip out on Santa to play ball.

"Hey, Earl Ed?"

He turns, the crazy light display dancing across his face. "Yeah?"

"Can I ride with you to your mom's?"

"Sure." He opens the passenger door to his truck, and I climb in.

My insides warm when he shuts my door. As much as I harp on how modern women should open their own doors, I actually enjoy it. The fact that he's doing so again also gives me hope that whatever gloom lingered over him earlier is gone.

Woody's lights glow in the back glass of the truck halfway down the road. I glance at Earl Ed as his face darkens when we top a slight hill and the lights dim.

"Your G-Maw's dumplings were the best I've ever had."

"Thanks, she's an awesome cook."

"Then why do people not like her tea?"

"Ever notice how she makes the main courses but leaves the desserts to the rest of the family?"

"Now that you mention it . . ."

"Let's just say when it comes to sugar, G-Maw has a heavy hand."

We share a laugh, and I lean a little closer to him. Our arms touch when he changes gears. My skin warms, and I mentally give myself the speech about how I don't need a relationship.

That's usually all it takes for me to focus on work and shut down any rogue butterflies trickling through my insides. But most guys I come across are all the same—

clean-shaven, sweater-vest-wearing executive types. Hallmark men.

If Earl Ed were in a Hallmark movie, they'd cast him as someone chopping down Christmas trees or sweeping sawdust in the main character's wood shop. Never the leading man.

But Hallmark isn't for everyone—including me.

We park near the edge of the yard, and he cuts the engine.

Earl Ed sighs. "Round three."

I raise my eyebrows. "I've got to admit, this is a bit exhausting."

"Yeah, imagine if my family didn't host it all. Some groups travel all across town."

"There's more of these?"

"Oh yeah."

I shake my head and stare at Carla's house. I can't decide if Southerners entertain to show off or to fellowship. After a week with the Mayberrys, I'm convinced it's both.

Earl Ed gets out and opens my door before I can think to pull the handle. He offers his hand, and I take it.

"Watch your step. This side of the yard is a bit bumpy."

"Thanks." I step slowly, but keep my hand in his. It's full of comfort and stability—two qualities often lacking from my life.

He holds it a split second before letting go to shut the door. My temperature drops with his release, then slowly picks up when he wraps an arm around my waist.

I allow him to lead me toward the lighted area of the yard. The motion lights sense our presence and start playing Christmas tunes. We've almost made it to the walkway when an older truck comes out of nowhere. Earl Ed pulls me into his arms.

We stand, frozen together until the truck parks. I exhale

and melt against him. Instead of letting go, he holds me tighter. Out of instinct, I lean my head against his chest.

"Look at y'all two all cozied up."

I jerk back from Earl Ed and see Paul strutting toward us. He's carrying a Styrofoam box. Whether it's the one from the other stop, I'm not sure.

He laughs and adjusts his belt buckle before opening the passenger door for Ms. Dot. Earl Ed and I exchange a look, then continue toward the front of the house. I brush my arm against his to see if he will wrap an arm around me now that we're in the light. He doesn't, but it's for the best.

We climb the wide porch steps and enter to Ziggy standing beside the doorway to the theater room.

"Hey." I'm a little shocked he's already here. How long did I stand outside with Earl Ed?

"We decided to use the theater room for interviews." Ziggy spreads his hands in front of him and stares off dreamlike. "It gives it that documentary flare."

I'm almost certain the network is shooting for homey Christmas instead, but this isn't the hill I want to die on. Besides, I'm part of a real holiday celebration for once and actually enjoying myself. Why ruin it by suggesting they move near the huge tree in the library?

"Great idea," I lie through my teeth.

A cute woman around my age slides in the front door and leans toward Earl Ed. A flare of jealousy sparks in me when she whispers something in his ear. He laughs and takes the dish from her hand, then walks toward the kitchen.

I follow him from a non-stalker distance. At least, what I assume is that distance. He puts the pan on the back counter and uncovers it.

I stand beside him and examine chocolate chip cookie dough. "What's that?"

He grins widely. "The cookie crack I told you about.

Jennifer knows I've been dieting, so she wanted me to get a bite before it's all gone."

"You've been dieting?" I mentally backtrack through the week. Nothing he's eaten made me think of dieting. Then again, in New York people try all sorts of fad diets, from liquid only to spraying their tongues with various flavors to try and satisfy cravings.

"Yeah, I used to be a real porker." Earl Ed slaps his stomach.

I cock my head, trying to imagine it. He's a bigger guy, but not fat. More along the lines of someone who might shop the big-and-tall store.

"Want a piece?" He pulls a cake server from a drawer and slices the edge of the rectangular cookie cake.

"Sure, I'll try it."

He smiles and cuts two pieces, placing them on the same plate. I choose to believe that he wants to share dessert with me rather than not waste another plate. However, he does get two forks.

I dig into my piece and take a bite. Sounds that make me blush leave my mouth. "Man, this is amazing!"

He nods. "And that's why we call it crack."

I finish my piece in record time, with Earl Ed laughing as I chew. He focuses on me until something catches his eye behind me.

"I'll be right back."

I lick my fork and watch him head toward the living room. Something touches my arm, and makes me jump. It's Carla.

"How do I look?" She turns slowly like a teenage girl in a scholarship pageant.

"Adorable." She's dressed similar to Mrs. Claus, but in a not so old and frumpy way.

"Great. Ziggy wants me to pass out cookies."

I scan the full kitchen as people trickle in. "Everything looks amazing, Carla."

"Thank you." She cups her hands on my shoulders and locks her eyes on mine. "For all of this."

"Of course. I'm just doing my job." Or I was. Then somewhere along the way, I started subtly flirting with your son and got giddy with holiday spirit.

Carla pinches my cheek like a nineteenth-century grandma. "You're sweet."

Desserts flood the many countertops as guests arrange their plates by similar items. "I'll go let Ziggy know you're ready."

Carla flashes her million-dollar smile, which I'm sure will make her an instant star among all the viewers of this TV special.

I go to the theater room and tell Ziggy she's in the kitchen. He and most of the crew follow me there. A few stay back with our interview setup in the theater room.

"I definitely want a good shot of all the dessert displays, especially her cookies on that center island," I say.

"Got it, boss." Ziggy turns on the camera and trails Carla as she works the room.

I stand back and admire all the sweets. Since we filmed her prepping for this in batches, I didn't realize how many cookies she actually baked and decorated today. There's enough to feed the town. Between that, the other desserts, and all the other courses served tonight, I can't imagine anyone in this town going hungry. At least not anyone who is friends with the Mayberrys.

A couple of older ladies nearby start chatting about Carla's cookies and how they swear she hides an ingredient whenever she gives out the recipes. I laugh loud enough to get their attention.

"Sorry, I just overheard what you said and thought it was funny."

"It's true," one comments, her beady eyes widening behind her glasses.

"You ladies are too cute. Would you mind letting me interview you for a few minutes?"

They exchange looks, then the one with the walker shrugs. "I'm past my prime, but now's as good a time as any."

"Great. Come with me." I lead them to the theater room, where Rambo left a mic and camera set up. Dougy is in the back on his phone. "Dougy, I need you."

He jumps to his feet and greets the older ladies.

"Let me shut this back door." I cross the massive room and pause when I reach the door near the movie screen. Muffled voices come from the hallway outside.

"You're the one who made the bet. You could've just let the inheritance play out."

"Like you would've given it to me anyway. We all know the whole having a family thing was your excuse to give the gun to Michael."

"Well, you had a chance to outshoot him and blew it."

"Don't act like you didn't cheer for him."

I stick my head out for a split second to confirm my fear. Those voices belong to Earl Ed and Earl Senior. I'm not sure what it's about, but that explains Earl Ed's sulky mood.

Earl Senior looks around Earl Ed at me. My throat goes dry as I duck my head in the room and shut the door. Then I march up the slight ramp toward the older women. "Who's ready for an interview?"

CHAPTER ELEVEN

Earl Ed

My entire body tingles as I stare at Daddy. "What are you looking at? Michael?" I snark to get his attention. He's glaring over my shoulder, eyes narrowed into tiny slithers like a venomous snake.

"No, smart butt." He blinks at me. "This immaturity is exactly why I'm close to Michael."

I cackle so loudly I sound insane. Daddy takes a step back as if he's scared of me. Not my best bet for convincing him to give me an antique gun.

"And Michael is mature?"

"He has a family and his own business."

I raise my hand. "Hello, Apple Cart County Business Owner of the Year right here, according to town hall. Also, might I add that Michael's family consists of a cocktail waitress and a baby whom he didn't father?"

"Yeah, well, it takes a lot more than being a biological

father to be a good dad."

I grit my teeth so hard I expect enamel to dust the hardwood floor. Did he of all people just say that? "You're right. Maybe you should take your own advice."

Before I say anything more hurtful that I might really regret, I turn and stomp down the hallway. My blood boils so hot that if it weren't for embarrassing Mama, I'd take off my shirt. I settle for rolling up my sleeves.

I'm almost to the front door when Woody pops out from behind a giant nutcracker and shoves the dogs at my chest. "Can you take the babies out for a poo? I don't want to miss Misty's performance."

I open my mouth to say "absolutely not," but before I can, he darts off in the opposite direction. I shake my head and take the tiny dogs out front and walk to Paul's truck. Maybe if they poop beside his door, it will get him back for almost running us over, always taking too much food, and just being himself.

While the dogs sniff his tire, I pace nearby and watch the crowd gathering around the firepit out back. Aunt Misty runs to the middle of the patio in a shiny dress. I guess Dolly Parton had her wardrobe change.

She asks for everyone's attention, and nobody listens. When she starts to talk louder, Uncle Joey tackles her and pushes her out of the light.

If that was the performance, I'm glad I didn't miss it. I laugh, releasing some of the tension I've held since leaving Daddy. I need to get out of here before I see him again. There's no way we can light candles at church tonight or kill a hog together in the morning until my temper mellows.

I walk back to Paul's truck for the dogs, but they're gone. "Taco, Belle," I whisper yell. Looking for two tiny chihuahuas in the dark is like hunting Easter eggs in a chicken coop.

A flash of green darts by, and I follow it to the light. It was Taco's sweater. Or Belle's. I'm not sure. Whichever it was, the other one is peeing on one of Mama's bushes.

"Stop that," I more yell than whisper this time.

I wait for the dog to lower its leg, then scoop them both up and hurry toward the house. Mackenzie stands in the front entryway with Dougy, packing up some equipment.

"Hey, Earl Ed. Do you mind taking me home? The guys are about done."

Perfect opportunity to leave. "Not at all." I literally drop the dogs. One lands on all fours and races off, and the other sort of bounces and yelps. I bend to pet it, but it scampers away, tail tucked between its legs.

I straighten to Woody staring at me from the hallway, hands on his hips. I turn to Mackenzie. "Ready?"

"Yes."

We make our escape in record time, and are halfway down the drive when I smell something. I sniff the air. "Do you smell something?"

Mackenzie winces. "Like a poop smell?"

"Yeah, must be a dead animal."

Her eyes widen as she cranes her neck to see up the road.

The smell doesn't go away. Finally, I pull over and open the truck door. When I get out to check if any roadkill is riding in our undercarriage, I see smooshed dog poop on my floorboard.

Sure enough, the bottom of my boot is covered in poop. "Ugh."

"What is it?"

I jerk the floor mat out and yank off my boot, then throw both in the bed of the truck. When I get back in, Mackenzie's face is full of questions.

"Are you okay?"

"I am now." I lift my socked foot. "I stepped in one of Woody's dogs' poop."

She laughs. I frown at her.

"Sorry." She pinches her mouth shut, and we drive to my place in silence.

Once we're parked by the basement, I climb out and jerk the floor mat from my truck. I pull it toward the spigot, then toss Mackenzie my keys. She balls up, and they land at her feet.

"Sorry. Let yourself in, and I'll be up after I clean this mess."

She unlocks the door, and I follow her inside to get some dish soap. When we make it to the ground level, she grabs my arm as I duck toward the kitchen.

"What?"

She stares at my face with a weird smirk on her lips. I study her brown eyes, watching her pupils dilate. Must be from the recent change in lighting. She takes a step closer to me. "Can we talk?"

"Uh." I glance down at my sock and behind me toward the door to the basement. There's poop all over my new boot and two-hundred-dollar WeatherTech floor mat, but when a pretty girl wants to talk . . . "Okay."

She leaves her hand on my arm and leads me upstairs. I stagger behind her, my one boot echoing on the wooden staircase like a pirate's peg leg.

When we reach my apartment, she leads me to the living area and sits on the couch. She stares at her lap and bites her bottom lip before speaking. "I overheard you fighting with your dad."

I lean back against the cushions and sigh. "Yeah, I'm not proud of what I said."

"About your dad cheering for Michael?"

"No, after that."

Her forehead wrinkles. "Oh, that's the last I heard."

I scratch the back of my neck to try and calm the nerves firing in it. I haven't known Mackenzie long at all, but I've spent a lot of time with her and trust her. She's also an unbiased third party, unlike anyone else I might talk to in a thirty-mile radius.

"I made a smart remark about Michael not being Colleen's real dad. Then Daddy snapped back something about how being a dad is more than fathering a child, and I told him to take his own advice."

She gives me the most pitiful face, like I'm one of those pets on the sad dog and cat commercials. All that's missing is Sarah McLachlan singing in the background.

"Michael isn't Colleen's father?"

That's not what I expected her to take away from this. "No, they got together while Krystal was pregnant by someone else."

Mackenzie wrinkles her nose. "That's weird. Like on a Lifetime movie level weird."

I nod. "Welcome to my world. Michael makes dozens of dumb mistakes, while I borrow a few Netflix DVDs and get caught. Daddy still favors him." I sigh. "I used to think it was because I was a fat linebacker and he was a wide receiver. Now I'm not sure what it was."

Mackenzie scoots closer to me and rests her hand on my knee. My leg warms at her touch. I mentally remind myself that she's friend-zoning me.

This has happened my entire life. Women hug on me, tell me what a good friend I am and how lucky they are to have me in their life. Then they ride off with some skinny dude like Bradley or Kyle—or God forbid, Michael.

It's like my whole life I've been one number away from winning the lottery of love. Actually, about seventy numbers if you count all the pounds I've lost.

I melt into the couch, preparing myself for her to say something sweet, then pull away. Instead, she leans toward me. Either I've shaped up way more than I'm giving myself credit for, or this woman is off her rocker.

My fears and fantasies all come to fruition at once when she touches my cheek and presses her lips to mine.

I stay petrified for a moment, afraid to move. Occasionally, girls will give me a peck on the cheek as a consolation prize, but I've never had one go for the lips.

As I'm waiting on her to pull back and giggle like it's nothing—because to the girls, it isn't—she tilts her head instead. Then she starts to kiss me. Like *really* kiss me.

Once the shock wears off, I wrap my arms around her and kiss her back. It's been a year since I've kissed a woman. Even then, it was a chick at some sleazy strip club Michael took me to in celebration of getting out of jail. She tasted like cigarettes and cheap wine. Mackenzie tastes like chocolate.

My mind bounces between trying to enjoy the moment and wondering when it will all end. *Will she jump back and say it's all some kind of sick joke? That Ziggy's been hid all along, filming the prank?* If so, I commend her. I haven't been so committed to a prank since senior year, when we tipped all Mason Magill's cows, then tied his bull to the school sign.

At last I give in and turn off my mind. If this is a one-time kiss, I'm at least going to enjoy it. And that's what I do for about five seconds before my phone buzzes in my pocket.

Mackenzie moves her hand from my leg. "Oh."

I grin sheepishly. "That's my phone."

She sits back, her face flushed.

I curse under my breath and sigh. "I've got to go to church."

She nibbles her bottom lip. "If I'm making you uncomfortable—"

"No," I laugh. "I would love to stay, but Bradley has signed me up to light candles at the midnight Christmas Eve service. It's part of my community service arrangements."

"Oh, I understand." She sits back on the couch as I stand.

I lean down and kiss her forehead. "I promise, it's not you. It's me not wanting to ruin my parole."

She gives me a lopsided grin and nods. I grab my keys and stare at my feet. Then I go to my room for a new pair of boots before leaving a beautiful girl alone, in the dark, on my couch.

Hmm, maybe that would be worth going back to jail.

Mackenzie

I stare at the door to Earl Ed's apartment for far too long after it's shut. The soft glow of one lamp in the corner matches my mood. I'm in the dark as to how he feels about me and how I feel about him. Still, a small ember of light burns inside me. He ignited a flame that I didn't know existed.

One that has me questioning my current life choices.

Do I really want to spend the rest of my holidays working? Do I really have to live in New York to make movies and shows? Do I really want to stay single?

For the longest, I've assumed I needed to live near the action. Twenty years ago, that may have been true. Now, I simply meet with Arnie, then get whisked away to whatever remote location has the best tax incentives for filming or snowy hillside—depending on the budget.

Maybe I should've gone to church with him. I haven't a clue what a church in Alabama does, especially on Christmas Eve. I didn't even pack a dress to wear.

I sigh and walk to my room. I may as well get some sleep. It's almost midnight, and according to Earl Senior, the hog-killing festivities begin at daylight.

After changing into pajamas, I climb under the covers and lie on my side. The Christmas lights on the mini-golf course glow behind the curtain, so I turn away from the window. That still doesn't help.

I toss and turn for a short eternity before giving up and opening my laptop. Ziggy told me earlier he loaded some of the footage to the production database. The producer wanted to view some, and I may as well, too, since sleep isn't happening.

It loads at the speed of an elephant tiptoeing through peanut butter, thanks to the satellite internet here. I hook to my phone's hotspot, which speeds it to an elephant's walk.

While I wait for the videos to load, I pull back the curtain and sit back on the bed. Red and green lights twinkle from the golf course against a clear, black sky. I'm used to snow and streetlights everywhere, but also blackout curtains in my bedroom.

For a split second, I question what might've happened had I gone to church with Earl Ed. Would he sit happily with his arm around me in front of all his family and friends? Or would he keep it more professional? Most importantly, would he even want to put his arm around me?

The first video starts playing, and I turn my attention to the laptop. It's footage from the cow poop contest. I laugh way too loud at the crowd's reaction to the cow dropping a load. It's been a while since I've gotten that excited over anything, except maybe a full night's sleep.

Next, I watch the parade. I'm used to police on horses in

town, but not random citizens. There are also plenty of goats, ATVs, and tractors. Maybe this year was a farm theme. Some older man is dressed like a western Santa. I can't recall where I've seen him before. Oh wait, he's the real version of Carla's cowboy Santa cookies.

Another video has Dirty Santa at G-Maws, then there's plenty of Carla in the kitchen. The more I watch, the more I dread leaving. Never in a million years would I have chosen to come to Alabama, especially to a town this small.

If this holiday has proven anything, it's that I don't always know what's best.

I'm going to miss the slower pace of Wisteria and Apple Cart County. Even more, I'll miss the people. Everyone is so impersonal in New York, and I thought I liked it that way. I just didn't know what I was missing.

I close my laptop and the curtain, then curl back in my bed. I stare at the ceiling as I wait on my eyes to adjust to the dark. The front door opens, and I hear footsteps past my room.

Part of me wants to jump out of bed and go find Earl Ed. We wouldn't have to kiss, or even talk. I just want to be near him.

I toss my covers to the side, then stop myself before getting out of bed. What am I thinking?

Tomorrow is Christmas. We're shooting one more big scene, then wrapping for good. By this time tomorrow, I'll be in my own bed in my own apartment in New York.

It's not fair to me or Earl Ed to try and start something. His life is here with his family and business. My life is wherever the job takes me.

I need to be thankful it took me here for one perfect holiday season, and nothing more.

CHAPTER TWELVE

Earl Ed

I'm ankle deep in hog guts when the TV van pulls up at G-Maw's. By the time I got home last night, Mackenzie was in her room, and she was still asleep when I left this morning.

What little time I could've slept last night was ruined by memories of our kiss. The only conclusion I can come to is that it's an isolated incident. She feels comfortable with me, it was late and dark, and she was lonely. I just happened to be there at the right time when she needed someone.

That doesn't mean I'm her right someone.

I slice off another pork chop as Rambo and Ziggy come my way. Rambo's face turns a greenish-yellow, and he takes a step back. I would expect that reaction from someone like Dougy, but not a guy named Rambo who likely asked Santa for steroids.

Ziggy asks a few questions and scans the array of meat

cuts with the camera. I answer his questions and continue cutting, all while scanning the yard for Mackenzie.

I don't see her. However, I do see Woody and his dogs in matching plaid pajamas. Now, there's a Christmas card photo opportunity. I don't want to know what Aunt Misty's wearing. Especially after she showed up at church last night in her Dolly Parton wig.

Some of the kids from the next road over walk up with their parents. Each one is holding a notebook and pencil. Their mom homeschools them and counts the hog-killing experience as both a field trip and major part of their science grade each year.

The smallest one raises his hand.

"Yes?"

"When can we help?"

"You can help turn the grinder at the sausage station." I lift my knife. "Cutting pork chops is very dangerous."

He nods. An older girl asks about the hog's weight and how much meat we get off of it. I want to say "look around" for the meat answer. But even if she doesn't get sarcasm, I can't say something so rude.

"I would ask that man right there." I point the tip of my knife in the direction of Uncle Joey.

I can relate to someone in customer service with all the referring to someone else. Except for the fact that none of these kids have cussed me out or hung up the phone.

Mama stops by with a platter of cookies. The kids get excited and lose focus on me. "In a few minutes, you can come in the house and celebrate Colleen turning one. I have a pig cake, and everyone's invited."

The kids chatter amongst themselves and ask their parents' permission. I go about my cutting, content with Ziggy focusing the camera on the kids rather than me. They scatter after a minute, and Ziggy follows Mama.

"I'm never eating a pork chop again," a familiar voice says.

I lift my head to Mackenzie snarling her nose. "Nobody wants to see how the sausage is made."

"I thought sausage was over there." She nods toward Uncle Joey, who's instructing a homeschool kid on the meat grinder.

I take off my plastic gloves and laugh. "It is. If you'd like a tour . . . ?"

She shakes her head. "I'm good. I'm actually about to go to the birthday party inside."

"Let me wash my hands, and I'll join you." I grab the knife and step away from the meat. "Uncle Joey, chops are ready."

Joey leaves Liam in charge of the grinder to come collect the chops and package them. I'm not sure Liam should be left alone with electric blades and children, but it's necessary if I want to go with Mackenzie. And I do, very much.

Her eyes bug when I hold up the knife. It's worthy of a *Crocodile Dundee* movie prop, and the blood on the end only adds to its authenticity.

I snicker at her expression and head for the house. She stays a few feet behind me until we reach the front door. "Could you open the door, please?" I hold up my nasty hands.

She tiptoes to the edge of the door, far as she can get from the knife and still reach the handle. I slide inside, careful to hold the knife close to my chest.

"Excuse me, coming through." I shimmy past people best I can for a bigger guy with dirty hands and a foot-long knife.

One of the homeschool boys grins with missing teeth when he notices my knife. "Is that what we're using to cut the cake?"

"Uh, no." I drop the knife in the sink.

G-Maw frowns when it sloshes some of her dishwater on the counter. "Careful, son."

"Yes, ma'am."

I turn the sink on with my elbow and make sure to wash my hands on the side not full of soapy dishes. I dry my hands, then dry the water that spilled on the counter, making G-Maw smile.

Mackenzie stands in the corner of the room, watching the kids gather around the kitchen table. Colleen is in a highchair at the end, with Krystal and Michael on either side. When Michael looks at me, I nod and grin. No use in being mad at him. It's Christmas, and it's not his fault I have daddy issues.

Michael gives me his goofy smile, letting me know all is forgiven. Ziggy comes around the corner with Dougy and Rambo in tow. They get a close-up of Colleen and the cake. It's a two-layer pig with bright pink icing.

The kids lean across the table as Mama leads them in singing "Happy Birthday." Colleen sucks in a deep breath to blow out her one candle, then sneezes across the cake.

Adults moan as the kids slowly recoil from leaning toward the cake. Ziggy steps back and wipes the camera lens with the corner of G-Maw's tablecloth. Not missing a beat, Mama pushes a plate toward the cake and gently lowers the top layer on it.

"This part can be Colleen's smash cake instead."

Krystal smiles and pushes a small pig-butt cake in the center of the table. "Y'all can use the real smash cake to make up for it."

"Yes," the boy with missing teeth whisper-cheers.

I stand by Mackenzie while Krystal sets the top layer in front of Colleen. She giggles, then fists a handful of icing. All the kids turn their attention from the baby to Mama when she slices into the bottom layer.

She slides a piece on a plate, then another, and another. The kids grab their pieces and mutter "thank you" when their mom gives them a stern look.

Mackenzie seethes. "Did she really have to make a pig cake red velvet inside?"

"Too much?" I smirk.

"A little, given the day's events."

I glance down at her hand near mine on the countertop. My arm tingles as I inch closer and rest my pinky finger on her hand. Instead of taking my hand, she pulls away and grabs a pen from her back pocket.

Then she spins around and grabs a notebook from the counter and fans through pages. "Ziggy, what all shots did you get of the actual meat process?"

Mackenzie steps closer to Ziggy as he backs toward the corner of the kitchen. I palm the back of my neck, regretting having tried to hold her hand.

I stepped out of my comfort zone and took a chance. I didn't get her affection, but I did get an answer to my burning question.

The kiss was a one-time thing she did on impulse.

Mackenzie

I choke up a little after calling "cut" for the last time. Carla smiles, then takes a generous bite from the cookie she's holding. We all laugh and cheer.

"Join me." She fans her hand over the platter of pig cookies. We all take one.

I bite into an ear and try not to think about the slaughtered pig in G-Maw's yard. This cookie pig tastes like strawberries, and it's heavenly.

It's weird for me to eat sweets on set. I must say that Carla's cookies are worth it. As well as last night's cookie crack. Directing a movie about the "twelve cakes of Christmas" last year soured my appetite for sugary treats. I had nightmares of sugar plums dancing in my head for weeks after we wrapped.

Carla crosses the kitchen and wraps her thin arms around me. She squeezes me and rocks me side to side before letting loose.

"Girl, I'm going to miss you so much. Not only have you made my dreams come true, but you're just a sheer delight."

"Thanks." My face warms at her compliment.

I wish she wouldn't thank me until after the show has aired. I'm afraid she might not feel the same if they don't edit enough of the footage with Misty or the hog. Maybe I can send her a director's cut for Christmas next year.

Carla holds up her finger, then prances off to the corner of the room. She returns with a large gift box. "For you, sweetie."

"Oh, that isn't necessary." *And it could also be considered a bribe.*

"I insist." She smirks and shoves the box toward me.

My arms droop with its weight, so I set it on the counter to open it. I pull out a neck pillow and blanket. Beneath that is literally a picnic basket full of food. Everything from cookies to ingredients you'd find on a charcuterie board and an actual board in the shape of the state of Alabama.

"Carla, this is so nice."

She shrugs. "I think it's a shame you'll be in flight while everyone else is enjoying Christmas treats and relaxing."

I reach out and hug her tightly. She squeezes me back,

and I swallow back a tear. She's the epitome of a loving mother, and I've become very fond of her.

Speaking of fond . . .

I pull back from Carla and look outside for any sign of Earl Ed's truck. Of course, their lawn is so massive, it wouldn't be hard to miss it among the acreage and multiple recreational vehicles.

Ziggy and Dougy start breaking down equipment. I fold a tripod to appear helpful and hide my curiosity about Earl Ed.

He'd mentioned coming to his mother's house after the hog killing, but I haven't seen him. Maybe he's upstairs, or in the basement, or the movie room. I can't imagine he'd be up for a long distance relationship. I'm not even sure if his parole allows him to leave the state.

But that kiss wasn't a mistake. At least not to me. If so, I would be able to forget about it and move on. But I can't.

We've formed a unique friendship over the past week, and he's the most genuine person I've ever met. He's also the first person with facial hair I've kissed. Unless you count the weird saxophonist who had a soul patch. I don't.

After our kiss, I think I prefer beards. I'm not willing to go full-on *Duck Dynasty* or Santa Claus, but there's something masculine about a man with a full yet trim beard.

We take the equipment out to the van. The motion lights start playing as we pass, and lights come on around the fountain out front. I spot Earl Ed beside a boat in the distance. As soon as I set what I'm carrying in the back, I head toward him.

"Hey."

He straightens from bending inside the boat. "Hi."

"What are you doing?"

He shrugs. "Checking something for Daddy. We're going fishing tomorrow."

"Oh." Now we're to the awkward part where the couple plays what I call confession chicken.

In movies, they each want to tell the other how they feel, but nobody wants to talk first. I've directed enough of these to know I'd be an idiot to get on a plane without telling him what that kiss meant to me.

"That kiss last night."

Earl Ed raises his palms. "Don't."

My voice cracks, along with my heart. "Don't?"

"Don't worry about it." He jumps over the edge of the boat and leans against the side. "It was late. We were both tired and alone at Christmas. I get it. You and me are great friends. There's no need to apologize for a kiss."

"Oh, okay . . ." I search his face for a sign that he wanted the kiss to mean more.

I open my mouth to say he's wrong, but all the logical reasons of why we shouldn't and can't date flood my brain. *Long distance. We met like a week ago. He votes Republican.*

Then I force down all the happy memories and many reasons why he's easily the most caring and uplifting guy in the world. I've learned a thing or two from watching actors all these years. Now, it's time for me to put on a show.

"Well, I'm glad we cleared that up." I fake laugh and shrug. He joins me in laughing.

I turn, then stop. "We better get to the airport."

"Yeah, y'all be safe."

Y'all? Did I miss the part when he retired as my official Uber driver for the duration of this job?

"Miss Mackenzie, are you ready?"

Earl Senior comes around the corner wearing a gun on his side and sunglasses on his face.

"Uh." I shake my head to snap out of a daze. "Yes?"

"Good. Earl Ed put your bags in my truck. I gotta run to

Birmingham and drop off some guns, so I offered to drive you."

I blink at Earl Ed, who's relaxed against the boat with his arms crossed. "Be careful."

"You too." Lamest goodbye ever, but what choice do I have?

I expected a love confession, or at the least a final farewell kiss. Not "be careful." He might as well have told me "good riddance."

Without so much as a hug, handshake, or even a high-five, I follow his dad to a massive Ford truck. I cling to the handle inside the door and climb up the step. A large leather seat engulfs me when I sit.

I never knew the inside of trucks could look so nice. Earl Ed's is top-of-the-line in my opinion, but it pales in comparison with Earl Senior's truck.

"What kind of truck is this?"

"Ford Raptor."

"It's nice."

"Thanks." He smiles and pulls into the drive. "The factory is a little more rugged, so I had a custom detail package added."

I nod.

"Your bags in the back seat in case you need anything."

"Thanks." I glance behind my seat. My eyes widen when I count at least five guns lined up on the floorboard beside my bags.

He laughs. "Don't worry. Those aren't loaded."

All the way to Birmingham, Earl Senior brags about his gun club and drops random facts about guns and gun laws. A few times, I'm certain I doze off. Or maybe everything he says just sounds so similar.

In order to travel on Christmas Day, I had to book several connecting flights, starting in Birmingham this time.

I suppose it's for the best, as it will shave off an hour and a half of gun history class.

We finally pull up to the airport. He hands me my bags and extends a hand. "It was nice meeting you, Mackenzie. You know I'm not a fan of your industry, but you're a nice young woman."

"Thank you."

He nods. "If there's anything you ever need from me, just let me know."

I start to walk away, but pause. "Actually, there is one thing you could do."

"What's that?"

I swallow and work up the courage to speak my mind. I may as well tell one Earl Mayberry how I feel about him today.

"You can be nicer to your son."

His mouth parts, and he takes off his sunglasses. Before he can talk, I continue.

"Earl Ed is a sweet, successful man, and he loves all of you dearly. I know he went to jail, but it's not like he killed someone or robbed the Pig or something. Give the guy some slack. We all have things we've done in the past that we're not proud to admit. Most of us have the luxury of them not showing up on a background check is all."

He sighs. Instead of waiting for him to respond, I turn and speed walk toward the airport entrance. That wasn't the speech I'd planned on giving, but it was still from the heart. If I can't be with Earl Ed, maybe I can make his life without me better.

CHAPTER THIRTEEN

Earl Ed

"Earl Ed!"

I turn to Big Mama rushing toward me, full force. She lands at my rib cage and wraps her tiny arms around me. Yep, her grandma name was chosen by my PawPaw as a practical joke. She's maybe a buck-ten soaking wet.

I pat her back as her gray hair catches on my beard. She steps back at last and scans me head to toe—twice.

"You're so thin, and handsome."

"Thanks." She's being generous with the word "thin," but I'll take it.

Unlike her, my PawPaw is a big man. Not in the fat sense, but what G-Maw calls big boned. It's safe to say I swam in his gene pool.

"How have you been? Your mama says business is good."

"Yes, ma'am. Going great. I've been working six days a week except for holidays since I started."

She pats my chest. "Good, good." A mischievous smirk crosses her face. "Good business, good looking. Any ladies in your life?"

"No, ma'am." *At least none I want in my life.*

I'd love to have Mackenzie in my life, but that offer is off the table. In fact, I'm not sure it was ever entirely on the table. More like sitting under a heat lamp, getting stale while I waited on her to place an order.

Maybe hot girls making out with me is equivalent to them hugging on me in high school. They've gotten more desperate with age. If I hold out another decade, maybe one will marry me.

"Steaks are ready." Daddy holds up a large platter, calling our attention to the back door.

He was in charge of grilling meat while Mama, Carly, and I handled all the side dishes and desserts. I offered, but he insisted that there are three things in life a man should never share—his wife, his underwear, and his grill.

Daddy crosses the kitchen and brings the steaks to the counter. I push a pan of buttered bread toward him. "You can throw this on for a minute or two. It will make it crispier than the oven."

He stares at the bread like it's a Democrat at a gun convention. If he burns the baguettes, that's on him. I offered to help with the grill.

"Big Mama, would you like a drink?" I ask.

"Sweet tea with lemon would be divine."

I busy myself fixing her a drink, while Daddy stomps off with the bread. Big Mama sips her tea and follows Carly as she sets the dinner table. She questions Carly on everything from boys to cheerleading to prom dresses. I think this is why we don't get with this side of the family more. Big Mama is exhausting.

About the time all the food is ready, Aunt Sheila's family

shows up. Her daughters look like they jumped out of one of those Disney tween shows. They're twins, but polar opposites. One plays ball and can scare you with her facial expressions. The other does pageants all the time and has worn fake nails since she was potty trained.

I don't know them well since they were little when I went to jail. And it's not like Aunt Sheila brought preschoolers along whenever she'd drop me off a care package. They suck to Carly and show her something on their phones.

"How are you, Earl Ed?" Aunt Sheila smiles at me. She's the slightly younger version of Mama with longer hair.

"Good, how are y'all?"

"Busy."

"I hear that."

Her husband, Rusty, walks in the kitchen, his phone to his ear. He's a dentist, and she runs his office. Rusty hangs up the phone and looks our way.

He shakes his head as he shoves the phone in his back pocket. "Looks like I'll have to go in early tomorrow. One of Jeffrey's boys broke a permanent tooth playing ball."

Aunt Sheila rolls her eyes. "Again?"

I laugh, and Rusty chuckles. "It would be funny to me, too, if those rednecks weren't cutting into my hunting time."

For once in my life, I'm thankful to have Woody as Aunt Misty's current husband. Sure, he's quirky and simple-minded. But at least he's not making Taco and Belle play travel ball over Christmas.

"I think we're about ready to eat," Daddy calls as he brings in the bread.

"Aunt Sarah isn't coming?" Carly asks.

"No," Mama, Aunt Sheila, and Big Mama say in unison. The aggravation in their tone is thicker than G-Maw's tea.

"She promised to FaceTime later." Big Mama pouts.

"Okay, then." Mama claps her hands and smiles, as if

trying to turn the mood in the room. "Everyone else is here, so let's pray and eat."

She nods to Daddy, and he goes into his usual speech-prayer. PawPaw removes his cap and holds it over his heart. Rusty "amens" whenever Daddy mentions guns.

With both sides of my family like this, I really had no chance of becoming anything other than a redneck. That's what happens when people marry within their county.

"Carly, can you help me, dear?"

"Yes, ma'am." Carly breaks away from her pre-teen fan club and stands by the glasses.

Yes, actual glasses. We drink from red Solo cups at G-Maws. This side of the family drinks from heirloom china. Daddy sometimes fusses about how bougie Mama is, but I think he secretly likes it. Using real dishes and having the house decorated like *Southern Living* fits well with his redneck-rich vibes of boats, trucks, tractors, and landscaping.

Carly takes drink orders, and pours everyone a glass. We're probably the only place that serves Diet Coke and sweet tea in goblets. Well, except for the casino where Krystal used to work.

Everyone gathers around our massive kitchen table with their drinks and sits in front of a place setting. There's a plate we can actually eat on with a giant silver plate underneath it, multiple forks, and Christmas decorations weaved around the food platters. Maybe we are bougie.

I should've known that when I asked the security guard to order me mint sprigs for the jailhouse kitchen and he looked at me like I had three heads.

"There's no hidden cameras lurking around here, are there, Carla?" Rusty cuts his eyes around the room as he lops a huge scoop of potatoes on his plate.

"No, they left earlier today and took everything with them."

Including a part of my heart. I pinch myself for thinking something so sappy. *Man up, Earl Ed.*

"And not a minute too soon," Daddy adds.

PawPaw laughs. "You've got more restraint than me, Earl. I couldn't have stayed in the house with cameras this long."

Daddy gives Mama a tight-lipped smile. "The things I do for love."

She rubs his arm. "Now, it wasn't that bad. They never even filmed you."

"So they say," Daddy answers around a mouthful of steak.

"Oh, honey. They wouldn't lie."

Daddy balks. "Mackenzie's a downright sweet girl, but all those city-folk types prey on people like us."

"What do you mean by that?" Mama's mouth drops, whether from shock or offense, I'm not sure.

Daddy wipes his mouth with the snowflake-print cloth napkin and sighs. "Carla, I agreed to it because I knew how much it meant to you. I have no doubt people will love you and your cookies. But you've gotta consider all they saw and filmed. The hog killing, the county parade . . . my sister."

Mama shrinks back in her chair. "And they can edit it how they please."

Daddy nods. "Afraid so, darling. There's nothing we did personally to embarrass the family, but as for our town as a whole and Misty . . ." He shakes his head. "They can easily *Duck Dynasty* this show and portray us as crazy rich rednecks."

Big Mama puts on her classic "bless her heart" face. "Earl has a point, dear. Why do you think we didn't visit earlier this week?"

Mama's face goes from shocked to confused. "Because you were working."

Big Mama laughs. "No, sweetie. I got off three days ago."

A few years ago, PawPaw retired from the fire department and Big Mama left the Apple Cart hospital to do travel nursing. They spend most of their time on the Gulf Coast. She works, and he fishes.

Mama turns to Sheila. "What about you and Rusty?"

Aunt Sheila hangs her head. "We didn't really have the flu."

"You lied?"

"Sheila didn't want to hurt your feelings," Rusty adds.

"I can't believe you would miss your daughters in the parade!"

Aunt Sheila swats a hand in front of her. "They'll be in more. It wasn't worth the risk of getting on camera."

Mama cups her hands under her chin and sighs. "Am I making a fool of myself with this?"

Everyone chimes in with their version of "no" to reassure her.

"We don't mind you being on TV. We're proud of you, Carla. We just don't want to be on it." PawPaw reaches across the table and pats her arm. His gray eyebrows thread together as he pulls his hand back and several green branches from the centerpiece drag across his plate.

"Like your daddy said, there's nothing wrong with you having a cookie show. But these TV people like to play up stuff for ratings. If we're not crazy, they'll find some crazy to throw in. Mackenzie, though sweet as a peach, may have buttered us up to open up our world to her. For all we know, she made us trust her to get all the juicy footage she could," Daddy says.

My stomach churns, and it's not from all the holiday food. I take a drink of water to try and settle it. That doesn't work.

After a few non-judgmental questions from Sheila and Big Mama about what cookies Mama made for the show, the conversation turns to hunting, fishing, and who everyone thinks will win the Super Bowl. Usual family stuff.

I try my best to join in and give my opinions on football and catfish bait. My mouth may can move past the TV show, but my mind can't. Mackenzie is a constant fixture in my brain that pops up when I least expect it. Kind of like a Cracker Barrel sign on the interstate.

Daddy's last words ring in my ears. For all we know, she may have played us all to gain trust. If so, that would explain the kiss.

Mackenzie

Finally. After a Starbucks and more than enough time to check all my emails and scroll social media, they call us to board the plane.

Nothing says "Merry Christmas" quite like traveling alone with two connecting flights.

I'm on the last leg of my journey and should be at my apartment door by ten. If everything goes well. You never know with airports.

I shrug my carry-on over one shoulder and my purse over the other. The employee checking tickets greets everyone with a smile worthy of a toothpaste billboard. She's way too happy for someone working at the airport on Christmas.

Aside from a handful of stragglers, I'm one of the few traveling alone. The young couple in front of me is almost sickening with their snuggling and googly eyes. I want to hit the guy in the back with my bag the second time he holds up the line to kiss her on the head.

Once I make it to my seat, I buckle my seat belt and close my eyes. A peaceful moment passes, then I hear giggling beside me. I open one eye and turn my head.

You've got to be kidding!

It's the happy little couple I got behind walking in. They stalled on the way to the plane, and I passed them.

I roll my eyes and turn my head toward the window. Then I dig in my purse for my headphones. As soon as this puppy's in the air, I'm plugging in a podcast.

The flight attendant does her usual spiel about safety and introduces the pilot. I try and focus on her voice rather than the kissing noises behind me.

Especially since the kissing noises remind me of kissing Earl Ed.

My chest burns as I imagine what the Mayberry family is doing now. It's only been a few hours and I already miss them—miss him.

This is my quickest flight, but it drags on for an eternity. I'm tortured externally by the kissing beside me and internally by thoughts of never seeing Earl Ed again.

Maybe Carla can come to New York for the premiere of her show . . . and bring her son. Ugh. That's a year away. He could be married to some Wisteria chick by then.

I shove my head against the seat and sigh. What is wrong with me? I never pine over a guy. Even worse, I've known this one less than two weeks.

It has to be my age. I see this all the time. Career women getting into their thirties, then suddenly wanting a relationship and family. That makes more sense. It's not him, it's me. More like my expiring ovaries, but still me.

I close my eyes and promise myself I'll be more open to relationships. That should help this aching inside me.

As soon as we land, I hop up with my carry-on and purse in hand. "Excuse me," I say sternly to the couple. They're too caught up in examining one another's interlocked hands to even notice me. I hike a leg over their legs and stumble into the aisle.

I hear Christmas music play over the speakers of the airport as I enter the terminal. More of my kind are present at the baggage claim section. The single, workaholic types who travel on Christmas alone, because to them it's just another day. At least we can function without someone glued to us like the couple that made my flight a nightmare.

I find my bag and exit as soon as I can. Snow flurries trickle down, hitting my face. I stop and button my coat at the sudden chill. The weather reminds me more than anything that I'm not in Alabama anymore.

Once I weave through tons of people for my Uber, I realize it even more. The driver introduces himself, then faces the road and falls into traffic. I sit in the back, watching the Christmas lights blur out the window as more snow falls.

My apartment building, though outlined with white Christmas lights, appears drab compared to all the places in Apple Cart County. Even the Piggy Wiggly is more festive.

I thank the driver and walk to the building, dragging my rolling suitcase behind me. Several people get on and off the elevator while I ride it to my floor. They're all carrying some sort of dishes or gifts. My guess is they've had Christmas with someone in the building.

When I open my own door, the lack of holiday spirit hits me like a ton of bricks. I have no tree, no lights. Only a lone poinsettia my mother bought in early December. Knowing her, it wasn't to be festive, but because it's the only plant she could keep alive this time of year.

I drop my bags in the hallway and bend down, expecting my cat to come. She's nowhere to be found. "Ryan Gosling," I call, peeking into the hallway, then the kitchen.

Yes, I named my cat Ryan Gosling. It started as a joke so

that when people asked if I had a roommate, I could tell them Ryan Gosling. Now I realize that just makes me sound like a delusional stalker. Even worse, Ryan Gosling is a girl.

"She isn't here," my mom calls from the living area.

I enter the room to one of those cheesy old soap operas on the TV. To get her full attention, I sit in the chair across from her before answering. "Isn't here? What, did she have a hot date tonight?"

"No, she ran away."

"Ran away!" My shoulders slump.

Ryan Gosling is a cat I rescued from the dumpster at a nearby Chinese restaurant. I'd toyed with the idea of having a pet for a while. Then, one day on impulse, I spotted a cat behind the restaurant. I've always heard cats don't last long in those types of environments, so I took her.

"Why would she leave? I gave her food, shelter, and vet visits."

"Must be the vet visits," Mom says nonchalantly, then downs half a glass of wine.

"Well, did you even look for her?"

"I called her, of course, and kept an eye out, but no sign of her."

"Did this happen today?"

Mom shakes her head. "The day after you left."

"And you didn't think to tell me?" I fight to control my voice. The last thing I want is to fight with my mother on Christmas.

"I knew you were busy, and then I left for my cruise and sort of forgot about her."

I balk.

"What? You haven't had her that long."

I sigh and mumble to myself, "What kind of life do I have that I can't even keep a stray cat?"

"What's that?"

"Nothing. You need anything?"

Mom downs the rest of her wine and licks her lips. "Not now."

I half-smile and try not to compare her to Carla. It's hard, especially since I imagine Carla sipping eggnog in front of one of her many trees.

I stand and kiss Mother on the head. "Merry Christmas and good night."

She stares at the TV and doesn't say a word. I drift down the hall to my bedroom and collapse face-first into my bed. I must've gotten on some kind of permanent naughty list at one point to have a Christmas this depressing.

CHAPTER FOURTEEN

Mackenzie

The train wreck that was Christmas is now over, and all of New York is settling into a normal routine. Well, New York normal.

I sit in the front office of the network responsible for Carla's cookie show, waiting to meet with the producer. The last time we met in person was before I left for Alabama.

My hands shake as I fumble with a loose string on my coat. The lobby is otherwise empty aside from a tank of exotic fish. I stand and stare at a red one with long fins to try and settle my nerves.

"Mackenzie?"

I straighten to find a young woman standing at an open door.

"Follow me. Kristine is ready for you."

I thread my fingers together and abandon my fish friends to meet with the woman responsible for my last paycheck.

When the receptionist stops in front of an open door, I suck in a breath. Maybe she likes what I did.

"Come in, Mackenzie."

Kristine stands, the desk almost to her chest. She motions to a chair in front of her, then climbs onto her office chair. The feminist part of me adores how such a tiny female can hold such a powerful position at a network.

I sit slowly as she motions for the girl to close the door on her way out. Maybe that's a common practice of hers, and not meant in a negative sense.

"First of all, I love the story you captured of Carla and her community."

I let out the breath I'd been holding and relax my shoulders. "Thank you."

"Her cookies are exquisite, and I appreciate all the thoroughness you took with getting unique shots. It's hard to believe you haven't worked for a food production before."

I laugh. "Well, I've directed quite a few movies where the heroine was a baker."

She laughs, and I laugh nervously with her. "Well, it shows. Good work."

"Thanks."

She steeples her thin fingers and taps them together. "As for the overall show, I'm thinking we can play up the redneck-town angle."

"I'm sorry, what?"

She rests her palms on her desk and shrugs. "You know, make sure to include how backwards some of their traditions are."

"Backwards?"

"Maybe that's too strong of a word. Let's see . . . more like outdated."

"What's outdated?" My blood boils as I prepare to defend the Mayberrys—and possibly all of Apple Cart County.

Though odd at times, these people have become like family to me. And every family has at least a few nuts on the family tree.

"The hog killing for one. Then there's the whole cow poop thing."

"That actually raised a lot of money to help needy children."

"And we will make sure to mention that."

Gee, isn't that generous of her.

"I'm thinking Misty will play a major role in every episode."

"Why?"

"For ratings, of course. She's by far the most entertaining of anyone there."

I wipe my hands down my face. "I thought we wanted to paint Carla and her cookie business in a positive light?"

"We did—we do. We will."

I cock my head, not fully convinced by her politician answer.

"Carla is great. However, you can only do so much with a picture-perfect baker in a well-kept house."

"Trust me, I know." Last year's movie, *A Cupcake Christmas*, comes to mind.

"It's the perfect combination. Carla will bring in all the traditional viewers wanting unique desserts. Then they'll talk about Misty to their friends, and all the non-foodies will watch, too." Kristine smiles and rubs her hands together like she's an evil, miniature mastermind.

I shrink back against the chair, intimidated by someone half my size. Not only is she a TV executive, but she's also the one who's paying my rent this month.

"Mackenzie, I really enjoyed working with you, and you've done a great job. I'd like for us to do more projects if you're open to it."

I open my mouth to answer, but stall. Do I say "thank you" for her offer, or do I spout off my vision for Carla's cookie show? One where Misty is simply a passing shadow or blurred out totally. I would, however, keep her step-dogs. Everyone loves a tiny dog in a sweater.

Kristine blinks. "Did you hear me?"

"Yes, I did."

She sits back in her chair and sways slightly. "But you're not interested . . ."

I slump down and sigh. "Kristine, I would love nothing more than to continue working for your network."

"But you don't agree with my decisions for the cookie show?"

I shake my head. "I'm sorry. Maybe it's from getting to know this family so well, but I can't allow them to be embarrassed like that."

Kristine sighs and raps her fingers on her desk. "Tell you what, send me your cuts, and we will make ours. I'll consider them both."

I smile.

"I can't make any promises, and there's a good chance I may not use any."

"I understand, but I do appreciate you working with me on this."

Kristine returns my smile. I stand to walk out, and pause when she continues to talk.

"A word of advice?"

I turn and nod.

"We meet a lot of interesting, and often kind, people in this business. You can't let your emotions come into play with reality shows or you'll never create a successful project."

I glance at the carpet, then back at Kristine. "Thanks."

"Sure thing. I'll be in touch."

I smile, then open the door and head down the hall. My

smile fades more the farther I walk. I live less than a mile from the studio, so I forgo a ride this time.

Sleet pellets dot my face and coat, which is even more annoying than snow. I tug my collar higher and fold my arms tightly. The cold takes over my mind for all of two minutes.

Then I'm back to thinking about Apple Cart, the Mayberry family, and of course, Earl Ed.

Why didn't I say something more when I left? Oh yeah, because he basically told me to take care of myself in the way you tell someone you never plan on seeing again.

Whether by intention or assumption, it still stung. Even worse, I'm the idiot who didn't at least hint that I'd like to see him again. I'm terrible when it comes to building relationships.

No wonder Ryan Gosling ran away.

Earl Ed

I was brought here against my will.

Okay, so that's not entirely true. I did agree to meet Michael and Krystal at Waffle House for brunch. But I almost cut and run, as G-Maw calls it, when Krystal announced she brought me here to meet her friend.

Colleen drools onto the tray of her highchair and whines.

"Here, baby." Michael wipes her mouth, then drops a Sweet'N Low packet on her tray. He turns to me. "She's teething."

She grins and sticks it in her mouth. I glance at Krystal, who smiles approvingly. This must be a common thing for them to do. I don't know much of anything about babies, but I don't think I'd give them a packet of sugar to chew on.

But it's their kid, and Krystal has her shirt on. That's enough reason for me to ignore this situation.

"Prissy should be getting off her shift soon. Then she'll join us." Krystal wiggles her eyebrows at me.

"Prissy? Is that short for Priscilla or something?"

"No."

"A nickname?"

Krystal shakes her head. "It's a real name."

"Okay." I force a fake smile to hide the fact that I disagree with that.

"What kind of waffle you gettin', Earl Ed?" Michael asks.

"I plan on sticking with bacon and eggs."

"Oh now, why would you come to Waffle House and not eat a waffle?"

"Uh . . . because you guilted me into coming?"

Michael laughs, mistaking my deadpan response for humor. I guess being sarcastic all the time has finally backfired on me.

A skinny waitress comes to our table.

"Hey, we're ready to order." I hold out my menu for her to take.

She laughs, then raises her eyebrow at Krystal. Both Krystal and Michael laugh with her. Then Krystal swats a hand at me. "Oh, Earl Ed, stop teasing."

I take a sip of my water and glance at Michael for an answer. He laughs louder, then turns to the waitress. "Have a seat, Prissy."

I choke on my water when I hear that name.

"Ah, quit coughing and scoot over for her, Earl Ed."

I cough even louder when I realize I'm likely the only person in here who knows the Heimlich maneuver. This is how I'm going to die—by choking to death in the Waffle House.

Prissy shoves me toward the wall as I chug some water in between coughs to catch my breath. "You okay?" she asks after sitting beside me.

"Yeah." I clear my throat. "You have very pretty teeth." I'm not sure why I complimented her smile, but it is nice.

Of course, so was Mackenzie's smile, which I've not yet managed to forget.

"Thanks, they're fake." Prissy licks her top teeth as she removes her Waffle House hat and sets it on the table.

I blink, unsure of what I should say.

Her hair is pulled back to where I can't tell the length but it's blond on top and brown on bottom. Sort of like a skunk effect, except all the way across instead of just down the middle. Her face is pretty enough, but she's super tan—like to the *Jersey Shore* girls level tan—and her skin is starting to show wrinkles. The most prominent feature I notice is a barbed-wire tattooed around her thin bicep. I bet there's a story behind that.

"Prissy, Earl Ed is Michael's cousin I was telling you about." Krystal beams.

"The one addicted to panty catalogs?"

Kill. Me. Now. More like, kill Krystal now! Of all the things she could've said about me.

Krystal at least has enough sense to see the error in that, because she mouths a "sorry" my way. Then she looks at Prissy. "He owns the Double Drive place not far from here."

Prissy scans my face, then tilts her head. "That's cool, but are you into Victoria's Secret or not?"

I scratch my neck, which is burning like I have chicken pox on steroids. "Not currently," I finally say to get everyone's eyes off me.

"Bummer," Prissy snips before taking a huge sip of *my*

water. If this is her way of subtly showing she wouldn't mind me kissing her, then she needs to find a less invasive intrusion of my personal hygiene.

The older lady who brought us drinks almost half an hour ago tiptoes toward our table. "Are you guys ready to order?"

"Yes, please," I answer.

Michael and Krystal go first, ordering for themselves and Colleen. I order eggs and bacon.

The waitress glances over her glasses at Prissy. "You eating with them, hun?"

"Sure." Prissy throws her hands up and orders some special meal. Then she nails my ribs with her poky elbow. "Don't worry, I get one free meal a day with my employee discount." She winks. "I saved today's for our date."

How fortunate am I?

Krystal starts spouting off more facts about me. None of which I want anyone to know. Of course, she leads with jail time, followed by my recent dieting, and how I haven't ever had a serious girlfriend.

Michael chimes in now and again with an embarrassing childhood story. As if going to jail for mail fraud and using Uber to make ends meet while I got my business going wasn't bad enough, we had to bring up my fat-kid days. So what if my lineman career started in kindergarten, or if G-Maw couldn't always find clothes in the husky section for me to match my cousins? There's no point in bringing that up now, here, in front of a girl they want me to date.

Yet, none of this seems to deter Prissy. Should I be relieved or worried?

"Just so you know, I don't judge nobody for going to jail. My ex was in there twice." Prissy leans closer and whispers in my ear, "Nothing reignites a fizzling flame like a conjugal visit."

I jerk away when her breath tickles my ear. However, what she says scares me even more than how she said it. My water dumps onto my lap and splashes on Prissy. She slides out of the booth and shakes out her wet apron.

I take the opportunity to exit the booth as well. "Sorry about that, y'all. Prissy, I guess we'll have to take a rain check." I nod at the water continuing to drip onto the seat. "No pun intended."

In a panic, I reach for my wallet and retrieve a twenty. I hover it over the table, but decide it might melt there. I hand it to Prissy instead.

"This should cover my meal and the cleanup."

Colleen coos at me, then laughs. Before anyone over one can comment, I bolt for the door and hop in my truck. If this woman is interested in me after that debacle, she's either a major saint or a messed-up sinner. Either way, I had to escape.

If there's such a place as purgatory, it exists inside the Wisteria Waffle House.

CHAPTER FIFTEEN

Mackenzie

"So, what do you think?"

I stare at the blank screen and prepare to scrape my jaw off the floor. The producer's cut is like *Redneck Island* had a bake off . . . and Misty beat out Carla.

Kristine and her entire staff stares my way, anticipating my answer. For better or worse, I can't leave them hanging.

"Wow. That should skyrocket your ratings."

They cheer and clap and high five one another as if they've won a leg lamp. Nobody cheered when we watched my cut. Although a few people did tear up during the Angel Tree scenes. Too bad we couldn't legally film any of the kids. That would really drive the point home.

Maybe that's the problem. If they can't go full-out tear-jerker, they'll just go full-out jerks. And they wonder why reality TV has such a sleazy reputation.

"That's the plan." Kristine's smile stretches across her face. "I'm so glad you could join us for the viewing."

"Yeah, so am I."

Am I? That response slipped out automatically like change from a vending machine. Why didn't I stand my ground on what I think? Make Kristine shake me down before I spit out change.

She sets the TV remote on the conference room table and nods toward the door. "Walk with me?"

I follow her down the hallway to her office. The entire walk, I try and drum up courage to not nod and smile at whatever she throws my way, like I'm a show pony at the county fair. Not that I've been to a county fair, but I've filmed a few movies that included them.

I'm certain Apple Cart County has fairs. Maybe I could go back when they have one.

"Have a seat." Kristine circles her desk and hops back in her chair.

I try not to smirk at the thought of her legs dangling behind the desk. She settles in and smiles at me.

"I have another unique reality opportunity."

I raise my brows, afraid to ask what.

"It's a documentary about the New York City ballet."

"Oh." That doesn't sound so bad. I doubt she can put a redneck spin on ballerinas. "Tell me more."

"I'm glad you're interested." Kristine clasps her hands together. "We really want to dig deep into the backstory of the ballerinas."

I nod. "Like how and where they grew up, and how they got to where they are?"

"Exactly." She clinches her teeth. "There's so many layers to these women. You wouldn't believe how many still struggle to pay their rent or battle bulimia to keep performing."

I lean back, and my limbs go numb. Maybe not a

redneck spin, but still a negative connotation. At least when I worked with Hallmark, everything had a happy ending. Often too predictable, but always happy.

"You're not with me on this, huh?"

My face must have ratted me out. I swallow and prepare to hold on to my vending coins. "I don't think we should expose their personal struggles."

"Mackenzie, you've got to realize that reality TV is all about reality. That includes the good, the bad, and the ugly. That's why it's so addicting."

I sigh and drop my chin in my hands. My limbs slowly gain feeling, because now they're burning. I raise my head and laugh at the absurdity of it all. I could make enough working with Kristine for a few years to start producing my own films. But I don't think it's worth it.

Time to shake loose of that money I've been holding on to so tightly.

"How about we make a documentary on reality TV?"

"I'm listening."

I white knuckle the edge of my seat. She didn't get my sarcasm, but she will now. "We could dive into the ugliness of taking good people and making them look bad."

This time, Kristine's jaw drops.

I stand, metaphorically shaking loose a pile of pent-up quarters. "Kristine, I appreciate the opportunity, but I'm going to pass."

I turn and let myself out. Though tempting, I fight the urge to glance back at her when I close the door.

A heavy weight lifts from my shoulders as I march down the hallway and out to the parking lot. I'm now an empty vending machine, both metaphorically and literally, since I turned down my biggest cash cow.

For once in my life, I went with my gut. All my life I've acted out of fear and done whatever necessary to advance my career, keep Mom and me in the apartment, or make others like me.

Today I did what I felt in my heart was right.

I start toward my apartment, excited and a little anxious about my next move. I haven't worked on anything aside from two small commercials since December. It's nearly February, and I really need something lined up.

I pull my phone from my pocket and call Arnie. He answers on the first ring.

"Mack, how's life treating you?"

I laugh.

"That bad?"

"No, not really." I hold my head high, realizing that I really don't have any reason to complain.

Except for maybe that my mom has started doing Zumba in the living room while I'm trying to sleep, and I never found Ryan Gosling. Oh, and there's the tiny inconvenience of everything reminding me of Earl Ed and Alabama. Aside from that, I'm great.

"What can I do for you?"

I blow out an icy breath, almost regretting my next words before I say them. "Do you know of anyone looking for a director?"

"I do, and they actually asked about you."

I perk up, and my steps lengthen. "What did you say?"

"I told them you were meeting with Kristine's company about some things so I didn't have your availability yet. Then I told them I didn't think you'd be interested anyway."

"Why would you say that?"

"Because you looked me in the eye and said, 'Not another Hallmark movie.'"

I pinch the bridge of my nose. "You're joking, right?"

"Wish I was, kiddo, but that's what I said."

"What did they say?"

"They said that's a shame, because you do great work."

"Have they found anyone yet?"

"Not sure. I can give them a call back, but you're not going to like it."

"What is it?"

"Let's see."

I continue my quick pace as I listen to him shuffle papers and mumble to himself.

"Okay, here it is. *The Thirteenth Cake of Christmas*."

"You're joking."

"Nope. It's the follow-up to that twelve cakes movie you directed before. They're filming in Vancouver. This time the baker's half sister falls for the man who tried to put her out of business before."

"Let me guess, she's a baker, too."

"No, no." He flips a page loudly, and I hold back the phone. "Says here she's a ballerina."

Well, shoot. If that isn't a sign. I laugh a bit hysterically. A woman passing me pulls her child closer and gives me a concerned glare. Maybe I am going crazy, but I'm for sure going to Vancouver.

"I'll do it."

"Wait, I haven't even talked money or told you when it starts."

"Doesn't matter. I need all the change I can get." And I mean "change" in every sense of the word.

Mackenzie

CRAZY RICH REDNECKS

The worst part about Vancouver in February is you never can predict the weather. It's usually raining or snowing, but you never know which until that day.

This week we have rain. After dictating what props and tricks to use so the bakery windows look snowy rather than drippy, I decided to save some exterior shots for later. We're now filming inside the ballet studio.

If there's one thing I hate worse than Christmas movies, it's Valentine's movies. This movie somehow includes both. It starts at Christmastime with a meet-cute at the bakery.

The guy comes by expecting to find the sister, then finds the new girl filling in while the sister is on her honeymoon with the flannel-wearing logger who won her heart over the store-closing sweater-vest man.

Ironically, sweater-vest is now wearing flannel with a thermal vest in an attempt to woo the woman. When she isn't there, he woos the sister.

"More?" My assistant, Trish, holds the box of Cheez-Its my way.

"Thanks." I grab a handful and chow down as they giggle to one another.

In this scene, she's at the theater practicing when he surprises her. I concentrate on the big picture—which is my job, but I'm mainly trying to keep from zoning out. The dialogue is almost word for word what I've heard a million times. He compliments her. She blushes and combats the compliment. He brushes something away from her face. I eat more artificial cheese.

It's a dance I've done a million times.

During my third handful of Cheez-Its, something catches my attention. The guy asks her to stay in his small town.

She immediately comes up with all the reasons why she needs to live in the city to pursue her dreams of dancing on the big stage. I find myself hanging on her every word as she offers a convincing argument. Everything she needs is in the city.

"But I'm not there, and I need you." The guy stares into her eyes, and she bats her lashes a few times before they share a PG-passionate kiss.

"Are you crying?" Trish whisper-yells.

"No." I sniffle and choke down the unruly teardrop trying to break free. "I have allergies." I clear my throat and yell, "Cut. Take a quick break."

The actors and cameraman give me puzzled looks. It's unlike me to call "cut" mid-scene. I usually keep the cameras rolling, Clint Eastwood style.

I set my clipboard on the director's chair and speed walk toward the makeshift office. My boots click on the wobbly boards haphazardly placed to create a dance studio space. I enter the office and shut the door.

Before I make it to the desk, tears fall. I slump into the chair and bury my head in my hands.

My life isn't sad because my mom is quirky, or because I haven't yet broken into making life-changing films, or because Ryan Gosling refused to live with me. Nope, my life is sad because *I'm* sad.

I'm the one making me sad. How pathetic is that?

I can't blame Hallmark, or Mom, or even the cheap cat food I thought would be sufficient to keep my pet satisfied. I only have myself to blame.

That love scene made me realize I've also blamed Earl Ed. For so long, I fantasized that he might come after me. If not on my way to the airport, then at least by New Year's. Instead, I rang it in with ramen noodles and box wine, wearing my pajamas. Pathetic as that sounds, my only other option was going to Coney Island with Mom and Arnie.

I'm going to die alone. Just like the poor ballerina sister thinks she will until the middle of the third act. I can overcome this sadness, but first I need to get past Earl Ed. That's harder said than done.

A quiet knock raps on my door. I wipe under my eyelids and suck in a breath before answering. "Come in."

Trish enters with a roll of paper towels. "I thought you might need these."

I sigh. "Did anyone else see me crying?"

She shrugs. "Maybe."

I arch a brow.

"Okay, so the people right around us."

I arch both brows.

"Okay, okay, you got me. Everyone saw it. I'm sorry."

I shake my head. "It's not your fault."

"We get it, Mackenzie. You're tired. We're all tired. If I have to pull apart cotton like fake snow one more time, the sheep I count to go to sleep will need to be sheared."

I laugh through a few stray tears, then reach for a paper towel. It's a new package, and the Brawny man stares back at me with his bearded grin. That's all it takes to make me lose it.

Trish circles my desk and wraps an arm around my shoulder. "It's okay. I didn't mean to stress you out more by reflecting my stress."

I blow my nose loudly, then whimper. "It's not you." I point a shaky finger to the guy on the broken wrapper. "It's him," I whine.

"The Brawny man?"

"Uh-huh." My voice jumps about three octaves.

"Did you direct that photo shoot or something?"

I laugh and cry and cough all at the same time. Trish squats beside me, her auburn eyebrows threaded with worry.

"It's a long story." I glance at my watch. "And I don't have time to tell you now."

"Maybe after we wrap?" She pats my shoulder.

I nod. "Let's just say they don't call Alabama the Heart of Dixie for nothing."

"I'll take your word for it." Trish stands slowly. She must really think I'm crazy now. "Want more Cheez-Its?"

I stand and pull off about five feet of paper towels to hopefully last me until the next break. "Please."

"Whatever you say, boss."

I give Brawny one more glance and try not to think about what the real Brawny man is doing right now. I hope he's thinking of me.

CHAPTER SIXTEEN

Earl Ed

In big cities, couples go to dinner and dancing or maybe some kind of show on Valentine's Day. In Apple Cart County, they come to Double Drive for a night of glow-in-the-dark mini golf.

This is my first time offering an after-hours round of golf with intimate lighting, but it won't be the last. Tons of people have come through and it's only ten. Instead of closing early to have paintball wars with my friends, I need to stay open until midnight more often.

I step onto the green to greet some of the newer customers and hand out vouchers for a buy-one-get-one milkshake deal. Paul and Ms. Dot walk by in matching heart sweaters.

They greet me, and I hand Paul a voucher. "Take this inside for a free milkshake."

His eyebrows shoot up. "Free?"

"Yeah, one free milkshake with the purchase of a milkshake."

His eyebrows retreat into a crossed mess. "Wait, I gotta buy one to get one?"

"That is the universal definition of buy one, get one."

Paul tosses the coupon over his shoulder and snorts. "Well, that ain't free, then." He wraps his arm around Ms. Dot. "Come on, Dot." He leads her toward the next hole, then looks over his shoulder and snarls at me.

I guess to the man who freeloads food every chance he gets, my milkshake coupon isn't a deal. I bend to pick up the coupon he tossed before another couple makes it to the hole.

"Earl Ed!" I straighten. Where have I heard that voice?

Sure enough, it's Prissy. Her hair is now brown on top and blond on bottom. She's with Michael and Krystal. By the stupid grin on both their faces, I assume this is another attempt at a setup.

"Hi, buy-one-get-one milkshakes?" I pass Michael a coupon, then Prissy.

She fondles my hand as I pull it away. Obviously, my subtle hint of giving her a coupon rather than buying her a milkshake failed to register.

"I was hoping you could come out to Broken Bridge with me later tonight. There's gonna be a bonfire and maybe some swimming." Prissy winks, and my skin crawls.

I don't want to picture her overly tanned skin in a swimsuit. She's too thin and wrinkled. Swimming with her would be like watching a shriveled sweet potato soak in a sink.

"I'm open until midnight tonight."

"No worries, the fun doesn't really start until then. That's about the time Pete comes over with the leftover queso and margarita mix from couples' night at Enchilada."

I close my eyes and take a deep breath. A decade ago, I might've been the first to jump off the bridge, then belch my way through second-hand Mexican food while I floated the river on an inner tube. Now, I just want to enjoy a peaceful night of managing mini golf, then cooking my own health-conscious quesadilla and watch *Stranger Things* in my boxers.

Is that too much to ask?

Another couple comes toward us, and I turn to Michael and Krystal, then Prissy. "Good seeing y'all, I gotta work."

I meet the couple halfway and hand the guy a coupon. He thanks me as I move on to the next couple behind them. Then I head inside the building to check on Carly.

She and her boyfriend, Andrew, are working the registers tonight. I cooked them a special Valentine's dinner in exchange for working the late shift for minimum wage. Not too shabby, especially since one of them alone can work circles around Liam. Thankfully, he's back at Auburn.

I greet those eating and check on Andrew, who's manning the concessions. "How's it going?"

"Good."

I closed the grill at ten, but left the concession area open for drinks and prepackaged snacks. One thing I learned is to never totally close a food station. People will eat all hours of the day. Take Paul, for example . . . although he literally eats into my profits.

Andrew hands Kyle his milkshake. Kyle shakes my hand before walking off. I can't help but notice he's only holding one. Maybe he will keep the coupon to bring a gal in soon.

"You need any help?"

Andrew laughs. "Yes, sir, that would be good."

"Don't sir me," I quip.

He blushes. "Sorry."

"No need to apologize. It just makes me feel old."

"Well, you are thirty."

I narrow my eyes. "I'd stop talking if I were you."

"Yes, si—" He clinches his mouth shut.

I laugh and slap him on the back. "I'm just messing with you." I stiffen my smile and point a finger in his face. "But don't mess with my sister."

He nods, and his eyes glaze with fear.

A middle-aged couple comes up with their coupon. Andrew sighs audibly. I'm also relieved to have a break in this conversation.

I take their order, and Andrew prepares two shakes. When they step to the side, my eyes land on perfectly straight, fake teeth. *Prissy.*

"Earl Ed, I'd like a moment of your time, if that's okay, before I head out to Broken Bridge."

I glance back at Andrew mixing shakes. Looks like he's got this covered. There's nobody else in line, and I'm running out of excuses. Maybe I should spill a milkshake on her since the water didn't work?

Prissy wiggles her eyebrows.

Ugh. Better nip this in the bud before it gets out of hand. "Come on." I motion for her to step behind the counter.

"I'll be back in a few, Andrew."

He nods while spritzing the shakes with whipped cream.

Prissy sneaks up behind me and snakes her slim arm around my elbow. My arm flares, and not in a good way. Maybe I'm getting a secondhand tanning burn.

Opening my office door creates the perfect opportunity to shrug her loose. I lead her inside and sit at my desk. Instead of sitting on the couch nearby, like any normal human might, she sits in my lap.

My knees buckle when her tailbone digs into my thighs. She wraps her hands around the back of my neck, and I swallow. Just when this couldn't get any more awkward, she kisses me.

My lips stiffen like cement. She fights for more real estate, but my mouth has an imaginary sign stating that

Mackenzie has a pending offer on the place. That sign is then guarded by an electric fence and large retaining wall.

I stand, causing Prissy to tumble down the retaining wall onto the floor.

"Ouch." She stands and rubs her backside. "What'd you do that for?"

"I'm sorry, Prissy. I'm just not interested in you like that." I sigh and frown.

She narrows her eyes. "It's because I work at WaHo, ain't it?"

"No, not at all. I make a third of my income off fried food."

"Then what?" She snaps her fingers. "I know, you met someone in jail."

"No!" I cross my arms, regretting even giving an ounce of care about letting her down gently. Emotionally, obviously, as I dumped her on the floor.

In my defense, the last thing to cling to me so tightly was a rabid squirrel wanting my almonds at a campsite.

"It's my hair, isn't it?" She flips her head, then tousles it. "You liked it better with blond on top?"

"No! Nothing is wrong with you, except that maybe you're a little aggressive for my liking."

She blinks.

"No offense. It's just . . ." I sigh. "I like someone else."

"The girl I saw you talking to up front?"

I slap my forehead. "That's my teenage sister."

"Oh."

"I like a girl who lives in another state. I know, that sounds so cliché and it will probably never work. But for now, she's the only girl I can think about. Heck, she's all I can think about. It's not fair to you or me or anyone else for me to try and date as long as I'm pining for her."

Prissy nods. "I get it."

"You do?" The shock in my voice echoes the surprise at her sudden change in mood.

"Of course. My ex talked me into getting this ring because he said it was more permanent than a gold one." She raises her sleeve and flexes the barbwire. "Later, I realized he was too cheap to buy real gold. He left me high and dry a year later, and I'm stuck with this awful thing."

"I'm sorry."

She chuckles. "Me too. Barbwire tats are for women who own Harleys. It took me years to finally get over him and get what I really wanted."

"Someone else?" I'm now curious as to what happened to the next guy. Did she smother him to death?

"No, this." Prissy spins around and pulls her jeans down a few inches.

I wince at a lower back tattoo—much lower than I'd like to see. Through squinted eyes, I make out what appears to be a butterfly landing on a dolphin with sparkles around it. So, essentially, a Lisa Frank tramp stamp.

"That's nice." Not really, but I figure the sooner I comment, the sooner she'll pull up her pants.

"Thanks, I think so." She jerks up her jeans and smiles.

I sigh, glad the peep show has ended. "So you understand why I can't date you?"

"I do." She flashes her white teeth and punches my arm with her fist. "Good talk."

"Yep." I rub my arm as she walks out of my office.

I wait a few minutes to give Prissy time to leave and my arm time to relax. Then I return to my post, humming that lame "Milkshake" song from my middle school days.

Earl Ed

. . .

Last night proved two things. One: My milkshake only brings all the girls to the yard when they're with their dates . . . who have a coupon. Two: I don't want my milkshake to bring any non-paying customers aside from Mackenzie.

When Carly, Andrew, and I finished cleaning up at one in the morning, I couldn't sleep. No matter what I tried, my mind kept circling back to the conversation with Prissy. That was the first time I confessed my feelings for Mackenzie out loud.

I don't think doing so made them more real, but it did make them more of an issue. It brought everything to the surface so that I'm now forced to deal with it. Like when you clean the back of the refrigerator and come across expired dairy products. You don't just shut the door and say you'll deal with them later. You get the junk out and deal with it then.

That's why I'm sitting in the county sheriff's office, waiting to talk to Bradley. Something I'd never do unless I was desperate.

"Earl Ed." Bradley walks in with a brown bag and removes his Maverick sunglasses. "What do I owe the pleasure?"

I want to say "cut the crap," but I actually need his help for once.

"I have a few questions concerning my parole."

"All right." He nods. "Come on in my office."

I follow him to his personal office, which is decorated with high school memorabilia, deer heads, and the road sign he won in Dirty Santa at G-Maw's house.

"Grab a seat."

He wasn't kidding about grabbing a seat. He points to a stack of camping chairs in the corner of the room before sitting in his office chair. I unfold one in front of his desk as he opens his bag.

Bradley pulls out a cheeseburger. I can tell by both the packaging and the bun that it's from Mary's. I've become some sort of food connoisseur for local eateries. Maybe I can expand my food knowledge beyond the county soon, which is where Bradley comes in.

"What's going on, big dog?"

"Okay, so I know I've been to Mississippi and Tennessee since getting out of jail. But those are bordering states and within the range of miles I was given upon release. What are my boundaries now?"

Bradley takes a big bite of his burger and chews while he stares above my head. He swallows. "You can't go to PCB, Earl Ed. We talked about this last summer."

"Still?"

Bradley nods. "Not unless you have a police escort." He grins. "Now if there's some kinda bikini competition you want to attend, I might can be of service to chaperone." Bradley laughs around a mouthful of food and wiggles his eyebrows.

"No. I was actually thinking of going the other direction."

"Oh, they have a bikini contest up north? In February?"

"No." This is as frustrating as talking with Prissy, but I refrain from making any smart comments since I need him. "New York."

Bradley's eyes bulge. "The state or the city?"

"Well, they're both in the state, but the actual city. Where Mackenzie lives."

"Wait, you're wanting to go visit Mackenzie?"

I sigh and nod. "Yeah. I need to tell her how I feel."

"For real, man?"

"For real. But I don't know how to find her, and I can't

go by myself." I grit my teeth and say four words I never wanted to say in a million years. "I need you, Bradley."

"Well, why didn't you say something earlier?" Bradley stands and slides his arm across his desk, pushing everything to the floor—papers, pens, his lunch. Then he rolls out a large map of the US across the cleared space.

I assumed we would just look it up online, but I get the sense this makes him feel more like a real cop.

"We need to search the area of NYC for all the production companies and film people." He draws a circle around the city with a red pen. "Then we can find out where she's working or where she lives. We can surprise her with roses, and candy, and you can get down on one knee."

"I'm not planning on proposing."

"Oh? Then why are you going to see her?"

"To tell her I like her and ask her out."

"Can't you just text that?"

I drop my head in my hands. "And we all wonder why he's still single," I mumble under my breath.

"What?"

"I said it will mean more in person."

"Oh, I guess you're right."

I shake my head. "Look, are you going to actually help me get to New York and look her up using actual online police records and stuff? Or are you going to sit around marking up a map like we're Lewis and Clark hoping to stumble across Sacagawea?"

Bradley rolls up the map and puts his hands on his hips. My hands tingle as I halfway regret going sarcastic. What if he kicks me out? Or better yet, messes with my parole?

"Aw heck." Bradley throws his hands in the air. "You're right. I just got caught up in the plan. I'm such a romantic at heart, you know."

No, I don't know.

"Give me two days to do research, plan to travel, and get my hat steam cleaned."

"Okay . . ."

"We'll meet here at eight hundred hours sharp on the seventeenth. Pack a blue button-down shirt."

I wrinkle my forehead. "Why blue?"

"It will bring out your eyes."

I blink. Creepy as that sounds coming from Bradley, I make a note to pack my blue-and-white-checkered Cinch shirt. This may be the only shot I have at starting something with Mackenzie. I need all the reinforcements I can find.

CHAPTER SEVENTEEN

Mackenzie

"What do you think of these?" Mom holds up a pair of lime-green shorts.

I wince. "Probably not the best idea for a woman pushing sixty."

She rolls her eyes and slams the hanger back on the rack. Why exactly did I invite her to go shopping? Oh, I didn't. She insisted we go shopping because my hotel room was "boring her to death."

Never mind the hotel pool and restaurant. She wanted to get out and see the town. All I want to do is rest these few days in between production. I thought inviting Mom to spend the weekend with me might be fun.

I should've known her idea of fun would be going nonstop.

"Where's that earring place you told me about?" Mom shuffles through a few more clothes way too wild for her age.

"It's down the block. A quick walk."

Leaving for the jewelry store is my best bet at sparing all of Canada from Mom's scrawny legs. Even though it's in the thirties here, I wouldn't put it past her to strut through the hotel in those shorts.

We stroll to the jewelry shop, enjoying a break in the drizzle that's been falling the entire time I've been here. Every day, either snow, rain, or a combination of the two has fallen. Until today. It's like the heavens are giving me a break, since I don't get the relaxing break from work I wanted.

"Did you remember to lock everything up before you left home?"

"Yes, and I turned off all the appliances, and even set out some milk on the deck in case Ryan Gosling shows back up."

I smile. "Wow, Mom. Thanks."

She swats my arm. "I'm not a child, Mackenzie."

"I know."

"Do you?" She laughs and shakes her head. "I wonder at what point did we switch roles. Was it when I moved in, when you finished film school, or even before then? You've always been so mature."

"Thanks." I wrap my arm around Mom's shoulder.

"I didn't mean it as a compliment."

I immediately drop my arm and twist my mouth.

"That's a great quality, don't get me wrong, but sometimes you need to have fun."

"Well, someone needs to be the serious one."

We enter the jewelry store, and Mom laughs. "I think you've got that role covered."

I snort. "Would you rather me not be responsible and make my own way?"

"No." She reaches out and pats my cheek. "I just don't want you to end up alone like me."

"You do realize you live with me, right?"

She nods. "And I got to live with Ryan Gosling for about two months." She shakes her finger and smirks. "And don't you think I didn't drop that line on my cruise."

Mom picks up a pair of bright pink flamingo earrings. I say nothing. Let her go wild with jewelry. Age appropriate or not, at least jewelry can't be responsible for her showcasing bony calves.

"Why did you never remarry?"

Mom sets the earrings back on the table and stares at the ceiling for a beat. Then she faces me and shrugs. "I don't really know. Looking back, I'd say I've always been more comfortable single than married. Your dad took off when I was pregnant with you, and we'd been married not even two years. Living with you and my mom felt natural. Now she's gone, but I still have you."

She wipes a stray tear from the corner of her eye. I wrap my arm around her again, and leave it this time. She snuggles me in for a quick hug. When we let go, I study her eyes.

For the first time, I make the connection of her living with Grandma. I'd always assumed Mom needed Grandma, but maybe Grandma needed her like she needs me. Mom has such a carefree spirit that it's hard to imagine her being the responsible one in an adult relationship.

She once called me from a cruise ship to check if she left her Spanx at home. After tearing apart her room, my room, and the laundry closet, I eventually found them in the microwave. When I called to give her the news, she cackled out, then said she'd forgot nuking them to try and increase the elasticity.

"So the only reason you're alone is because you're used to being alone?"

Mom shrugs and tries on an eccentric necklace. "In a way. After your dad left, I focused on having you and my job. Those, along with your grandma, became my main focus. If I were to have a relationship with a man, he'd have to somehow fit into the life I'd built already."

I nod. "Makes sense." Actually, a lot of sense. "I don't really make time for anything but you and work." I smile at her.

"That's not good, Mackenzie."

I swat her hand. "That's not fair. How is it you get to be fine without someone and I don't?"

"Because you're still young and you haven't even had a kid."

I cross my arms. "Not everyone has kids."

"You don't want kids?"

"That's not what I said."

Mom turns to the side and checks out her necklace in a display mirror. "I know it's not, but you're already *several* years older than when I had you."

I don't care for the way she drags out the word. Emphasizing "several" is like a backhanded way of saying "many."

"I'm fine with just us, really."

"Are you?"

I slant my eyes and frown.

Mom lifts a red rope necklace around my neck. "This looks great with your eyes."

"Don't change the subject."

"See what I mean? You're not fine. You're grumpy, and it's not because you're working a bunch. You're always working a bunch. Something else is up."

"I'm just bored with these TV movies."

She shakes her head. "Try again."

I take off the red necklace and toss it on the display table. "What do you want me to say, Mom? That nothing has been the same since I left Alabama? That I miss the slower pace of life and the people I met there . . . especially Earl Ed?"

"Yes!" Mom jumps, dropping a strand of beads on the tile floor. It makes a loud ping. *Several* people stare at us.

I bury my head in my hand and walk toward the corner of the room. She follows.

"Mackenzie, it's okay to feel something for a place, for a person. It's more than okay. It's normal!"

I unbury my face. "Not for me."

"Maybe going to Alabama showed you what you're missing."

"What's that?"

"A life."

I open my mouth to snap back, but she keeps talking.

"You need to be open to love and new opportunities. Just because you've always done something doesn't mean you can't change."

"I could say the same for you."

She fans her hand in front of me. "Go ahead."

"You know, you could date and find someone now."

"Maybe, but so could you."

"Touché."

We stare at separate earring racks a minute in silence. My mind wanders to my last day in Alabama, the one I've replayed like a broken record. Some nights I even dream of how it might've played out if I'd been honest with Earl Ed about our kiss.

"You wouldn't miss me if I went to Alabama?"

"It's not like you're at home that much now."

"True." I hold a pair of pearls to my ears. Carla would like these.

"Besides, if you decide to move down there, I know you'll take me with you."

I drop the earrings. They crackle as they hit every rack on the way down. *Several more* people give us the side eye.

"Let's go," Mom suggests.

I nod in agreement as she works on shedding all the necklaces she's tried on. Once we're stripped down to only what we came in wearing, we hightail it back to the hotel.

Earl Ed

"I told you this was a bad idea."

Bradley growls at me through clinched teeth. Or maybe he's growling at the TSA agent across the table from us. These two have carried out the longest staring contest in history.

"I am a county sheriff. I have a degree in criminal justice. From The University of Alabama!"

The man doesn't blink. His bald head reflects the florescent light overhead. I squirm in my chair and focus on his badge. What kind of name is Gilead? When his eyes slant toward me, I smile and silently pray that he doesn't do a background check on me.

Stupid Bradley.

He just had to pack a pistol in his carry-on. While I was chugging water and trying to deal with the overflow of people passing us in every direction, the TSA flipped out over Bradley's bag check.

Now we're in this small, white room that looks way too much like the jail visitation room. The only thing keeping me from a nervous breakdown is Bradley being the one on trial.

He straightens his Stetson and stares at Agent Gilead before spouting off more credentials for carrying a gun.

Gilead lets him finish, then leans forward, resting his

elbows on the table. "Look, hillbilly, I couldn't care less what you got from where. The only what and where I care about is that gun and this location. And they don't go together."

Bradley drops his head on the table and sighs. I never thought I'd see the day. The man broke Bradley.

"Your gun wasn't in a hard case, and it was too close to the ammo."

After a long pause, Bradley lifts his face. "Y'all used to be a lot more understanding. My buddy's married to the love of his life now because he brought her a stuffed deer at this very airport."

Gilead's jaw drops. "You know Jack Jackson?"

"Yeah." Bradley cocks his head my way. "We all grew up together."

The agent laughs. "He's a bit of a legend around here."

"Really?" I've gone from nervous to intrigued by how this dude knows about Jack.

"The footage of that deer is in all the new TSA training videos. My buddy even dressed up as him for Halloween."

"Like Jack?" I ask.

"No, the deer." Gilead almost cracks a genuine smile.

Bradley grins like the Grinch after he stole Christmas. That means he's up to something.

"Sir, Jack did that to profess his true love." Bradley slaps a hand on my shoulder and shakes me. "I brought my friend all this way to help him find his true love."

Gilead wrinkles his brow. "And you needed a pistol to help him find love?"

"No, sir, I needed a pistol because we're two rednecks planning to walk the streets of NYC for the first time."

"Not acceptable." Gilead grimaces.

Bradley sighs and drops his face.

After a little more back and forth, with Bradley only making it worse, we get out alive. They confiscated the pistol and ammo, but didn't run a background check on me. I call that a win. Even if Bradley did pout the entire plane ride to New York.

Bradley kicks the edge of the sidewalk as we wait on our Uber to Mackenzie's apartment. "This sucks."

"I tried to tell you."

"Why should I believe you? I'm your parole officer!"

"Shhh. People are listening." Random passersby stare at us like we've lost our minds.

Given the fact that we flew all this way to try and surprise a girl I've only known a short time and haven't seen in a few months, I'd say they're probably right. But Bradley doesn't have to announce to everyone in earshot that I'm an ex-convict and he tried to open carry in New York.

"You've got to restrain yourself, Bradley. This isn't Apple Cart County, it's the Big Apple. People aren't used to us."

"That's an understatement." Bradley crosses his arms and pouts.

My phone dings. "Cheer up, our ride is here."

An older model Chrysler car squeaks to a halt in front of us. We open the back door and smoke rolls out like a red carpet. I hold my breath as we slide in the back seat.

We stare at dreadlocks until the driver turns his head. He has a ponytail in his beard and a nose ring on each side of his nose, which is also blowing smoke.

"Welcome, I'm Runaldo. Did you guys enjoy your flight?"

Bradley reaches for his back pocket. I elbow him before he can flip out his badge. "Easy, cowboy," I whisper through clinched teeth.

He lays his hand in his lap and exhales through his nose. For a split second, I swear I see steam come out of Bradley's nostrils. Whether from anger or secondhand weed, I'm not sure.

"We had a good flight, thanks." I cough through the words, then crack my window.

If I can survive the setup with Prissy at Waffle House, I can survive this weed wagon for a few miles. I tilt my head toward the cracked window like a puppy. I'm tempted to stick my head out like a full-grown dog, even though it's freezing outside.

Bradley pouts like a kid who's lost his favorite toy. That's actually a pretty accurate description for him. Meanwhile, Runaldo turns on the radio and bobs his head to "Magic Carpet Ride," which I find fitting for this occasion.

After half an hour of hippie music and marijuana remnants, I'm almost high myself. I begin to open the door before he fully stops in front of Mackenzie's apartment complex.

"Thanks for the ride." I hop out of the car to what I'd hoped would be fresh air. It's not.

I'm used to hayfields and pine trees and morning dew. Not smoke, smog, and city. Still, it beats the smokestack we marinated in riding here.

Bradley is on my heels, cursing under his breath. He sniffs me like a dog as we enter the building.

"What are you doing?"

"Seeing how we smell."

"We ate Shoney's for breakfast, spent an hour in a tiny room with TSA, flew economy, then rode in a weed factory. How do you think we smell?"

"Good point."

Bradley leads the way to Mackenzie's floor and apartment. The closer we come, the more my nerves twitch. What will she think of me coming all this way? What if she doesn't care to see me? Even worse, what if she pretends to want to see me because she feels bad about me coming all this way?

Bradley knocks on a door, jerking me out of my daze. I

rock on the balls of my feet while we wait for someone to answer. This could be it.

A few torturous moments later, the door opens to an older woman with reddish-brown hair.

Bradley snarls his nose at me. "I don't remember her looking this old."

I slap the back of his head, and his hat falls off. He whines and bends to pick it up.

"Hi, ma'am, do you happen to know a Mackenzie Magee who lives in this building?"

"Yes, she's my daughter."

My eyebrows shoot up.

Bradley laughs. "That makes sense."

I ignore him and focus on the woman. "Does she live here?"

"She does, but she's working in Vancouver."

"Oh." My voice falls with defeat.

The woman's lips curve into a smirk. "Are you by any chance Earl Ed Mayberry?"

I laugh. "Yes, ma'am, I am."

"I'm Rosie." She offers her hand, and I shake it. When she lets go, she says, "Hold on a minute."

Rosie disappears, and I wait with Bradley as a woman walking two giant poodles in sweaters passes us. Bradley holds his hand out and coos, "Hey, poochy poos." The dog nearest us almost takes his hand off. I laugh as the woman shoves her nose in the air and hurries her dogs along.

Rosie returns with a folded piece of paper. "I just came back from visiting her a few days. This is the number and address to where she's staying."

"Thank you so much."

"No, thank you. She's been a pain in the tushy, all moping around ever since she came back from Alabama."

I shouldn't smile at that, but I do.

CHAPTER EIGHTEEN

Mackenzie

It's the last day of filming, and I'm counting down the minutes. Between Mom's quick visit and the epiphany of how much Earl Ed means to me, I've never been so ready to wrap filming.

After this job, I can hopefully visit Alabama for a few days.

Trish hands me a cup of coffee and sips one herself.

"Thanks."

"Welcome. Austin is in wardrobe. I told the stand-in to come run lines with Amelia so we can go ahead and set up the shot."

"Great idea." I turn to our ballerina love interest woman. "Hey, Amelia, let's run the scene with Austin's monologue."

"Okay." Amelia sets down her water bottle and stands on her mark.

Trish places the stand-in on his mark. *What happened to*

the guy we've been using? I sigh. He probably got an actual on-camera role and left for that job like most do. Wait a second . . . I must be going crazy, because the new guy looks just like the Apple Cart County sheriff. Although, I've never seen him without a cowboy hat.

I shake my head and blink. "Okay, let's run the scene."

The guy starts reading the script as the cameraman takes my spot, making adjustments. Now I'm really losing it because he even sounds like the sheriff. I shake off my delusions of doppelgängers and focus on the second cameraperson. I instruct her to zoom in when Amelia asks, "How do you feel about me?"

That's when it all goes rogue. The mystery man stand-in flips the page and reads something I've never heard before. Never from this movie, or any other.

"You're the one person who gets me. I know we're complete opposites. You're city, I'm country. You're sushi, I'm bacon. But somehow it works. Before I met you, I thought I may never find someone who truly gets me. Someone who likes me for me, despite all my flaws. And maybe you don't like me still, but I like you—a lot. Even though we're many miles apart, I'd like to see where this thing could lead. And that's why I wrote all this and sent it by Bradley, because my parole wouldn't allow me to leave the country."

"Cut!" My eyes bulge. "Bradley! I knew you looked familiar."

He grins, and my limbs tingle as I process what he just read. "Earl Ed wrote that?"

"Yeah."

"Why didn't he just call me?"

"He wanted to tell you in person, but he couldn't travel outside the country just yet."

"So he sent you?" My forehead wrinkles.

"Not exactly."

I glance at Amelia. She shrugs as if she's as clueless as me. "Amelia, take five."

She nods and walks toward the snack table. As confused as I am, I can only imagine what's going through her head right now.

I step toward Bradley. "What happened, then?"

"Earl Ed wanted to just call."

"Makes common sense to me."

"But I insisted on a grand gesture."

I roll my eyes. "You do realize I see these things all the time."

"Yeah, but I don't. My day-to-day is filled with busting up meth labs and writing tickets for four-wheelers crossing the highway."

Laughter fills my lungs, then I choke out tears. "Thank you. No matter how the message was sent, I needed to hear all that."

Trish steps up with a roll of paper towels. The Brawny wrapper is hanging by a thread, but she left it on. I look at his ripped-apart face and laugh through my tears.

"Where is Earl Ed now?"

"He's in New York at your apartment."

"Wait, what?" I expected to hear Alabama, or at the least the border.

"We went to New York first, but your mama told us you were here. I formed a plan, told him to write out what he wanted to say, and hopped on a red-eye."

Trish blushes. "He sweet talked me into standing in to get your full attention."

I shake my head. "You crazy people."

"So do you have a message to give back to Earl Ed?"

"Yeah, but I'm going to need to deliver it myself."

"I'm more than happy to relay it until you get back."

"Nah." I sigh. "We're done after tonight. Besides, it feels kind of wrong to have you pass along a kiss."

Mackenzie

After an exhausting day of flying—with Bradley—we make it to my apartment. No more than I was around him in Alabama, I could sense he had a big personality. I had no idea.

He talked my ear off the entire flight, flirted with every stewardess, let a little boy across the aisle wear his hat, and led our entire section of the plane in a game of "I Spy."

I turn the key and push open the door. My heart races as I enter the apartment, expecting to find Earl Ed. Instead, Mom is in the living room in cobra pose on a yoga mat. She's dressed like Jane Fonda in a color run.

"Mom, are those the lime-green shorts from that boutique?"

She stands and giggles. "Yes. I went back for them when you were at work."

I exhale, then glance around the place.

"He's on the balcony untwisting my water hose." She grins and winks at me. "You done well. He knows how to fix the ice maker and the toilet."

Oh my. I rush toward the balcony, not caring to know the story behind that. I slide the door open to Earl Ed holding a fat, furry cat.

"Ryan Gosling?"

"Sorry to disappoint you . . . unless this is some kind of role-play game." A flirty grin covers his face.

I laugh and point to the cat. "No, the cat is Ryan Gosling, but she ran away for a while."

He strokes her back, and she meows. "So that's why your mom's been calling her Ryan. I wanted to go with Cuddles."

I take a step closer to him and pet Ryan Gosling.

"She started hanging around the building, so I brought her up and fed her. She likes me."

I smile. "She has good taste."

He cocks the side of his mouth. "You think so?"

"I know so."

He stares at the cat, then slowly raises his eyes to me. "Did you happen to get my message?"

"I did." I grin.

"Did you read the transcription?" He rests his hand on mine. Ryan Gosling purrs when her petting comes to a standstill.

I nod. "Every chance I could in between Bradley's stories on the plane."

He chuckles. "Good. I had reservations about sending the village idiot, but he was eager to work and insisted I use his services."

"He got the job done."

Earl Ed locks his fingers with mine and stares into my eyes. "Good. I wasn't sure, since I'm still waiting on a response."

I step closer so there's nothing between us but Ryan Gosling. I drop Earl Ed's hand and wrap both my arms around his shoulders. Then I kiss him.

Almost like before—but better.

This time I'm not acting on impulse. I'm sure of my feelings for him, and I'm sure that he feels the same way about me. I kiss him like there's no end to our time together.

Of course, we still have the distance thing to work out. But the important part is that there is now zero distance in our hearts—or our communication. Man, it's great not having to go through Bradley.

"Meow." Ryan Gosling wiggles her way to the ground.

We pull apart, and I stare at her. She gives me a sassy look before trotting inside with her tail raised high.

"I guess she doesn't approve of us together?"

"I think she's just jealous is all," I assure him.

"Of which one?"

We look at each other after she's no longer in view and laugh. Then he scoops me in his arms and carries me inside the apartment . . . where Bradley has now joined Mom in yoga.

Earl Ed looks at them, then me, and keeps walking to the front door. "Want to get something to eat?"

"As long as it's not here," I answer, peering back at the weirdos.

"My thoughts exactly." He puts me on the ground and grabs my hand. We cackle all the way to the elevator.

I have no idea how this will work with us living so far apart and his temporary travel limitations. However, I've seen enough Hallmark movies to know that love will always find a way. Even if the girl has to leave the big city behind to start a life with her flannel-wearing lumberjack.

For once, that storyline sounds like the perfect plan.

EPILOGUE

Nine Months Later

Earl Ed

I stop in front of the guest bedroom door and knock. Mackenzie comes out and grins. She's still wearing black pants and shoes, but with a bright pink sweater and pink lipstick. By next Christmas, I plan to have her completely off black. Her mom even helped me devise a plan.

"You look beautiful, as always."

She stands on her toes and kisses my cheek. When she falls back on her feet, she clinches her teeth.

I rub her arms. "Are you cold?"

She shakes her head. "Nervous."

"Nervous? Why? My family loves you. They loved you last year even before we were dating."

She laughs. "Not them, the showing."

I wince. "Is it that bad?"

She shrugs. "It won't be for Misty."

"Oh Lord."

She sighs loudly.

"Well, you can fill me in on the way. You know how Mama is about being on time for events."

We head for the door, and I grab my keys and wallet from the now-finished kitchen counter. Christmas lights reflect on the granite from Mackenzie's tree. She decorated the apartment the first night she got in town.

Commuting hasn't been as bad as I'd anticipated. We stay busy with work and visit one another when one of us gets a break. I've become fond of her mom, Ryan Gosling, and many New York restaurants. It's freeing to have so many different food cultures in close proximity.

In Apple Cart County, we have barbecue and country cooking. The only thing close to ethnic is Enchilada, which I don't count as real food.

We climb in the truck, and I back out of Double Drive. Mackenzie takes my hand when I rest it on the console. I give her knuckles a gentle kiss, then lower our hands and listen to her recount the meeting with Kristine from the network.

My stomach tumbles a few times as she reminds me of details I'd forgotten by now. Aunt Misty dressing like a saloon girl to carol, Aunt Misty dressed like Dolly Parton for the progressive dinner, and about ten other Aunt Misty instances. Of course, there are a few Paul and Bradley sightings sprinkled in.

I give her hand a gentle squeeze and silently thank God that Misty no longer shares our last name. If we're lucky, they won't point out how close of kin she is to us.

A few minutes later, I pull up to Mama's house. She's

added even more lights this year—they stretch the length of the driveway.

Mackenzie turns down the radio, then her smile grows wider. "Nice touch having the music start out here."

I smirk. "I thought you didn't like Christmas music."

She lowers her eyes. "Well, I—"

"Uh-huh." I laugh as she turns toward the window.

I park close to the front and survey the other vehicles. All family. No Paul, Bradley, or the likes. That's a relief.

We go inside to chattering voices. I duck my head in the theater room to find the family mingling and passing around popcorn. Mama spots us and rushes to the door.

"Mackenzie!" Mama pushes me aside to hug her.

I shouldn't take offense, but she sees her every time she visits Alabama. And she saw her yesterday. At least they get along.

"You're just in time." Mama releases Mackenzie and balls her hands under her chin. "Come, get popcorn and find a seat." She fans her hands toward the front, where an old-time popcorn cart is set up.

I frown at the memory of putting that together yesterday. That popcorn better be good. We follow Mama to the front of the room.

"I'm so excited!" She smiles widely as a commercial ends and the show starts.

Mackenzie clinches her jaw in a fake smile, then slants her eyes toward me.

I cup my hand on the small of her back. "Why don't you find us a seat, and I'll get some popcorn."

She lifts one corner of her mouth. I rub her back, then march toward the popcorn cart. If it hadn't become one of my healthier go-to snacks, I would pass due to my animosity for the cart.

After filling two Christmas cartons of popcorn, I join

Mackenzie near the back. She's beside Lacie, who's propped her popcorn bucket on top of her pregnant belly. Collins salutes me from Lacie's other side, where he's holding two buckets. I'm assuming this is her craving.

I nod to him and loop an arm around Mackenzie when I sit. Words play across the screen, and everyone cheers when it mentions Mackenzie's name in the corner under "Directed By." She blushes slightly, and I kiss the red on her cheeks.

The next thirty minutes are a rollercoaster of ups and downs as the first episode plays out in front of us. It's mostly of our home and getting to know Mama. They zoom in on a family photo above our living room fireplace.

Mackenzie whispers in my ear around a mouthful of popcorn, "I added that shot to prove your dad is really in the picture."

I laugh. "Pun intended?"

She giggles nervously. I watch her react to a clip of Misty, then crane my neck to see Mama's reaction. She's all smiles, and Misty looks practically over the moon.

The final scene ends, and a teaser for the rest of the season plays across the screen. Clips of the cow pooping and Misty in her wig flash before us. I wipe sweaty palms down my pants and sigh. Mackenzie double fists the remainder of our popcorn and reaches for one of Lacie's boxes.

Then the credits play.

I hold my breath as the screen cuts to a commercial and Daddy hits pause. Mama stands and walks toward us. Mackenzie swallows and grabs my hand.

"Mackenzie." Mama sits in the empty row in front of us and tears stream down her face.

Mackenzie bites her bottom lip. "Carla, I'm so sorry. I didn't have final say in the clips. I—"

"No." Mama wipes at her tears. "These are tears of joy. I loved it!"

"Really?" Mackenzie's eyes bug, and she loosens her death grip on my hand.

Mama nods and cries more. Mackenzie stands and hugs her over the seats. I attempt to catch the popcorn bucket that falls, but fail. Kernels hit the floor, and the container rolls under the seat.

Nobody seems to mind, except for Lacie, who sighs, then mutters, "I was going to eat that."

Misty rushes up and wraps her arms around Mama and Mackenzie. They break the hug in record time.

"Ladies, this is so exciting. I can't believe we're going to be stars." Misty beams and does a weird little jig in her sequin heels.

Mackenzie puts on another fake smile. "I'm glad you enjoyed it, Misty." She bends and picks up the popcorn carton.

Misty starts chattering about all her favorite parts to a captive audience.

"Mama, Mackenzie and I are going to get a vacuum for this mess."

Mama's face communicates jealousy for not thinking of that first. I laugh to myself as Mackenzie and I exit the row of cushy chairs and leave her with Misty.

I lead her to the laundry room. "Feel better about the show?"

"Much." She sighs and scans the space. "I can't believe this is a laundry room. My first apartment wasn't this big."

"We also use it as storage."

"Do you think your mom might let me store some of my things for a while?"

I raise a brow. "Your things?"

She shrugs. "I might've looked into moving farther south lately."

I place my hands on her shoulders. "Seriously?"

She nods. "I'm sure my mom would want to move with me, but prices are better in the South. And the way I travel, I might as well live where I want."

"Which is?"

She smiles. "Close to you."

I pull her in for a kiss. It takes her a second to kiss me back as I can still feel her smile against my lips. I rake a hand through her hair and kiss her harder, then engulf her in a massive bear hug.

She giggles when I pull back enough to look in her eyes.

"What's so funny?"

She swallows one more giggle, then straightens. "It's a little funny, don't you think? Me moving to a smaller town for love. After all these years of rolling my eyes at Hallmark."

A commotion sounds outside the laundry room. I jolt to attention and turn toward the door. Taco—or Belle—runs by, followed by a baby goat, followed by Woody, who slips and falls on the marble floor, knocking down a Christmas tree.

I watch the train wreck, then grab the vacuum to take care of the popcorn, along with the glass ornaments Woody ruined. We stop in front of the mess, where Misty is fussing over Woody, who's worried about his dogs. Meanwhile, the goat is eating one of Mama's real plants.

I plug in the vacuum, then kiss Mackenzie on the cheek. "Baby, it's safe to say falling for me is nothing like Hallmark."

Sign up for Kaci Lane's newsletter to receive a free short story about Earl Sr. reconciling with Earl Ed.

A preview of the first book in this series is included after the Acknowledgments.

ACKNOWLEDGMENTS

First, I'd like to thank God for giving me creative ideas and placing the right people in my path to help see them to fruition.

My husband, Blake, gets credit next for always supporting my writing endeavors, even if he finds my stories a little too "girly and Hallmarkish." Of course, this book kind of broke the mold when it comes to that.

I also want to thank my readers and ARC team for their support. To all the people who read early, point out typos, post reviews, and cheer me on behind the scenes—You. Are. Awesome! I could not do what I do without my readers, and I love y'all!

Of course, I'd like to thank my editor, Joanne. She's always a pleasure to work with and polishes my books to help them shine. (FYI: She said this is her favorite book of mine so far!)

TRY THE FIRST BOOK IN THE SERIES
CHRISTMAS IN DIXIE

Lacie

"With a cold front moving in Christmas Eve, it looks like Atlanta might just get a white Christmas. So keep an eye on the roads. I'm Lacie Sanderson, on location in downtown Atlanta, wishing you all a safe holiday."

I put on the smile that helped me win Apple Sauce Queen my junior year of high school and wait for Dustin's signal. After an awkward minute, he nods, and the camera light stops blinking.

"That's a wrap, Lacie."

I immediately slump my shoulders and relax my quivering cheeks. "Thank God, it's freezing out here." That came out a little too southern, as does most everything I say when the camera isn't rolling.

"Well, you're headed west. Mark said the precipitation should fizzle out before it reaches Alabama."

I arch my eyebrow at Dustin. "No, it's going to move faster than Mark thinks. Alabama will have snow by Christmas morning, if not sooner."

TRY THE FIRST BOOK IN THE SERIES

Dustin shakes his head and chuckles. "Whatever you say, Lacie Bug."

I frown. He'll never let me live down the day my parents visited The Weather Channel and spilled the beans on my childhood nickname.

Dustin continues packing up his camera as I remove my earpiece. Once everything is put away in the news van, he wishes me a Merry Christmas and heads back toward the station.

I blow into my chapped hands and hop in my Honda CR-V. I turn on the heater and choose my favorite Christmas music station. It's only a few miles to my apartment, but it takes a half hour thanks to all the rush-hour traffic running both ways. I assume half the people are headed to work and the other half out of town. Over the past few years, I've met very few people in Atlanta who are actually from Atlanta.

After witnessing an exchange of horn honks and obscene gestures among my fellow commuters, I make it home. I've got to finish packing and make sure everything is in order so I can leave after seeing Collins. My insides warm, and I smile. Not the fake Apple Sauce Queen smile I reserve for on-camera, but my natural, not-so-over-the-top smile. Collins and I met on New Year's Eve last year and have dated ever since.

He checks off all my boxes. He's handsome, successful, smart, and compassionate, and he's been going to church with me. I can totally see us getting married one day. Which is why I've made every excuse under the sun to keep him away from my family.

As my G-Maw would say, they'd have him running like a chicken with his head cut off.

In high school, my daddy strategically cleaned his guns at the dining room table whenever a new guy would pick me up for a date. And he still says he can't understand why I broke

TRY THE FIRST BOOK IN THE SERIES

up with Bradley. Ugh. From leading our high school football team to win state to serving as the Apple Cart County sheriff, Bradley Manning has made the whole town of Wisteria, Alabama, practically worship him.

I roll my eyes as I hop out of my crossover and lock the door behind me. Daddy is the least of my worries. My extended family is the real reason I want to keep Collins under wraps until I lock him down.

I go inside my apartment and take a whiff of the air. I should probably wash my egg skillet soiling in the sink before I leave. When you have to get to work before six a.m., you learn to let a few things slide.

I drop my purse on the tiny kitchen counter and roll up my coat sleeves. As I scrub the yellow scales on my not-so-nonstick skillet, my mind wanders. I imagine walking down the aisle toward Collins in a beautiful gown, with my arm looped through Daddy's. Then my perfect day is ruined by my crazy Aunt Misty whistling loudly and bringing everyone's attention to her improper choice of wedding attire.

I wince as I rinse the pan. Yeah, we're definitely eloping. With any luck, I can keep Collins away from the full Mayberry clan at least until the ink on our marriage license dries. Then it will be too late for him to cut and run, as G-Maw would say.

I reach for my hand towel that reads, "Christmas Cookies and Hallmark Movies." I dry my hands, then spread the towel across the counter and set the pan on top to dry. The hand towel takes up half my counter space.

When I moved to Atlanta, my choices were get a teeny tiny apartment or a roommate. And since I knew absolutely nobody and I'm not claustrophobic, I chose Option A. I'm not a huge fan of the city, but working for The Weather Channel has been my dream since fourth grade, when Jim Vann visited our school.

TRY THE FIRST BOOK IN THE SERIES

In Alabama, we have a weird hierarchy of celebrities. There's Nick Saban, the Alabama football coach, followed by two heavyset guys who have a radio show about little more than food and corny impersonations. Then there's Jim Vann. He's the king of weather in the southeast.

I've watched him navigate us through every storm throughout my life. I've always had a fascination with weather, but when he visited my elementary school and showed us weather graphs and polygons in real time, I made up my mind then and there to become a weather girl. But not just any weather girl. I wanted to anchor the news for The Weather Channel. And with an on-camera position in the field, I'm well on my way to fulfilling that dream.

I remove my coat and lay it across my purse, then head to my bedroom. My suitcase is already open on the bed, with most of my clothing folded beside it. I walk to my closet and stand on my toes to rummage through the top shelf. Or more like the only shelf. If I don't take my own coveralls, I'll end up wearing my brother's skanky hunting clothes to the family hog killing.

As soon as I smoosh my coveralls in the corner of my suitcase, I change out of my work clothes. The last thing I want to do is wear slacks, heels, and a blouse on a four-hour drive to the middle of nowhere, so I exchange that outfit for my thickest sweatshirt and some yoga pants.

I check my appearance in the full-length mirror hanging from my closet door. There. A bulky Mississippi State sweatshirt to make my brother mad, along with slightly faded elastic-waist pants. The perfect attire for Wisteria.

Collins

TRY THE FIRST BOOK IN THE SERIES

My stomach churns as I get a text from Lacie saying she's done packing and ready for me to come over. I text back that I'm on my way and stare down at my own suitcase in the hallway.

She has no idea that I've managed to take off work and spend Christmas with her. I shrug on my jacket and slip out into the garage before my roommates ask any questions. They know I'm planning on visiting her family for the holidays, but they don't know my intentions.

I've known Charlie since rush week at Georgia, and he's sending vibes that he knows something is up. But I can't tell him or Mitch that I've had a diamond burning a hole in my pocket for several weeks now. Mitch would try and talk me out of marriage, as he's committed to nothing but noncommitment. And Charlie would act awkward around Lacie, since his weakness is keeping things on the DL.

I run a hand across my short beard and hop into my Land Rover. I feel a little silly dressed in scrubs, knowing I'm coming back here after leaving Lacie's. But she thinks I'm on call this weekend and that I'm going to the hospital after I leave her place. Lacie picks up on everything, which has made keeping secrets from her much harder than fooling the two goobers I live with.

We both live downtown, but I would like to buy a house in the suburbs once we marry. I know Lacie's only in Atlanta for work, and having a yard wider than my push mower might be a nice change of pace.

It doesn't take me long to get to her apartment building. I jump out and knock on the door. She answers right away and smiles up at me, her chocolate-brown eyes shining. I step inside and pull her in for a hug. She's warm and cozy and smells like flowers. I'm not sure what kind, but it's soothing. I've dozed off more than once on her couch while she snuggled up to me with her hair under my nose.

We both work crazy hours, but that's part of the commonality that kicked off our very first conversation. And her drive and ambition were a total turn-on from day one. Then her sweet-as-molasses voice sent me over the edge. It didn't take but a few months for me to know I wanted to marry that girl one day.

Lacie lifts her head and gives me a quick kiss before breaking the hug. I follow her a few steps to her tiny living room and take a seat on the couch. She plops down beside me. "Maybe you won't have to go in on Christmas Day," she says.

I shrug. With any luck, we'll be snuggled up at her parents' house celebrating our first Christmas engaged. "There's a good chance I will. I'm still the low man on the totem pole in surgery."

"Well, as someone who had to give a weather update at every fake Santa stationed in Atlanta last year, I can assure you working on Christmas isn't fun."

"But you had such a cheerful attitude doing it." I run my hand through her dark hair and smile.

"You didn't know me last Christmas."

"Not in person. But I still watched the weather." It was true. When I saw her at the hospital benefit on New Year's Eve, I knew right away she was the beautiful girl I'd watched deliver the weather every morning while getting ready for work.

Lacie leans back against my chest and sighs. "I'm gonna miss you this week."

"Yeah, and I'll miss you." I try to sound as if I'm not about to strike out toward Wisteria.

Lacie never says much about her hometown, except that it's small and she has a big family. It's probably one of those places with a gazebo downtown and Christmas wreaths on every streetlamp. Like in those low-budget Christmas movies I've suffered through the past month, all because I love her.

She raises her head and grins at me. "I better hit the road. The temperature is supposed to drop all day."

I chuckle and pull her close. "And you can't drive in the cold?"

She narrows her eyes at me. "No, it's gonna snow."

I laugh harder. "Okay, maybe here."

"No, in Alabama, too."

"Uh-huh." I nod my head.

She gives me the same face ornery patients do when I try and convince them that residents are real doctors. "Collins, I've been studying the weather patterns for Alabama all week. Trust me."

"Okay, babe." I raise my palms in surrender.

She stands slowly and reaches out her hand. I take it and stand in front of her, wrapping my arms around her small waist and pulling her in for a kiss. She fits perfectly between my arms, and all I can think about is how I can't wait to officially spend the rest of my life snuggled next to her.

After the kiss, I squeeze her in tighter, feeling her heart beat against my chest. It's all I can stand to not go ahead and propose right here, in her living room, while she's dressed in sweats and I'm in my scrubs.

But Lacie deserves better than that. She's old-fashioned and high-class. I need to meet her parents before I propose and let them know my intentions. Then I need to plan the perfect proposal. Someplace outside. Heck, maybe even in a gazebo. Someplace special, where she'll always remember that moment.

After a long minute, I pull away, knowing she's anxious to get on the road. "I'll put your bags in for you."

"Thanks."

I follow her to the door, where she has way too many

bags for a few nights. But she always overpacks. I've never understood that. I could go to the moon with only one suitcase.

I take her two biggest bags, and she follows me with a fancy duffle and her purse. I maneuver them all to fit best in the back of her crossover and close the hatch. She smiles and kisses me gently on the lips.

I smile back. "Merry Christmas, Lacie."

"I'll be sure to call you when I get there. Wisteria doesn't have the best cell service, so I'll call from Mama's. You'll have the house number that way, too."

I nod. "I love you."

"I love you, too." Her eyes sparkle as those words leave her pink lips. My heart skips a beat, and it takes everything in me to not jump in her vehicle and suggest we elope.

Instead, I run my hand down her hair and squeeze her cheek. Then I go to my own vehicle and drive back home. By now, my roommates are on their way to work, so I can get packed and head toward Wisteria.

My hand trembles as I fumble with fitting my key into the garage door. I'm going to a place I've only heard about, with no real plan of how or exactly when I'll propose. I'm thinking Christmas Eve, but the lack of certainty behind it all makes my mouth go dry. It's not like me to not have a plan.

I go inside and change out of my scrubs and into khaki pants and a buttoned shirt. My usual look outside of work. Then I get to packing.

After stacking my clothes and tossing in my toiletries bag, I fumble around the bottom of my sock drawer. There. I bring out the tiny black box and pop it open. The corners of my mouth raise as I admire my grandmother's diamond. As the only child and grandchild, she left it to me for my future bride. I've already had it sized to fit Lacie, thanks to sneaking one of her rings to the jeweler's.

I close the lid and exhale a huge breath. Then I tuck the box securely in the inside zipper pocket of my suitcase. I take a quick glance around my room to make sure I didn't miss anything, then head outside.

As I climb into the driver's seat, a knot forms in my stomach. I'm about to drive hours away to a town I have no idea about to meet people I've only seen in photos, then propose to the woman I love. But if it ends with Lacie promising to be my wife, it will all be more than worth it.

ABOUT THE AUTHOR

Kaci Lane is a journalist turned fiction writer who believes all stories should have a happy ending. While unsuccessfully trying to learn Spanish for a decade, she has become fluent in sarcasm, Southern belle and movie quotes. She is married to a Southern Gentleman and has two young children who help keep her humility in check. Connect with her on kacilane.com or Facebook.

BOOKS BY KACI LANE

Bama Boys Series*

Hunting for Love

Chicken about Love

Hammered by Love

Cutting out Love

Apple Cart County Christmas

Christmas in Dixie

Crazy Rich Rednecks

Schooled on Love Series

Taco Truck Takedown

Side Hustle

Buggy List

Off-Season

Books in Shared Series with Other Authors

No Time for Traditions

A Perfect Match in Silver Leaf Falls

*If you enjoyed the Apple Cart County Christmas books, revisit Apple Cart County with the Bama Boys series, starting with *Hunting for Love*. Set in Apple Cart, Alabama, it includes secondary characters from the Christmas series.

www.ingramcontent.com/pod-product-compliance
Lightning Source LLC
LaVergne TN
LVHW041630060526
838200LV00040B/1517